YELLOWSTONE BEAR TALES.

BOOKS BY PAUL SCHULLERY

Old Yellowstone Days (editor)
The Bears of Yellowstone
The Grand Canyon: Early Impressions (editor)
The Orvis Story (with Austin Hogan)
American Bears: Selections from the Writings of Theodore Roosevelt (editor)
Freshwater Wilderness: Yellowstone Fishes and Their World (with John D. Varley)
Mountain Time
Theodore Roosevelt: Wilderness Writings (editor)
The National Parks (editor)
Island in the Sky: Pioneering Accounts of Mount Rainier (editor)
Wildlife in Transition: Man and Nature on Yellowstone's Northern Range
(with Don Despain, Douglas B. Houston, and Mary Meagher)
American Fly Fishing: A History
Bud Lilly's Guide to Western Fly Fishing (with Bud Lilly)
A Trout's Best Friend (with Bud Lilly)
The Bear Hunter's Century
Pregnant Bears and Crawdad Eyes: Excursions and Encounters in Animal Worlds
The National Parks: A Seventy-fifth Anniversary Album
Yellowstone Bear Tales (editor)

CONTRIBUTING AUTHOR

*The Sierra Club Guides to the National Parks: The Rocky Mountains
and the Great Plains*
The Adirondack League Club 1890–1990

YELLOWSTONE BEAR·TALES

edited by

PAUL SCHULLERY

ROBERTS RINEHART, INC. PUBLISHERS

Copyright ©1991 by Paul Schullery
Published by Roberts Rinehart, Inc. Publishers
Post Office Box 666, Niwot, Colorado 80544
International Standard Book Number 0-911797-98-X
Library of Congress Catalog Card Number 91-60434
Printed in the United States of America
Designed by Linda Seals

Yellowstone Bear Tales
is dedicated to Marilynn and Steve French, and
to the good work of their
Yellowstone Grizzly Foundation

CONTENTS

Part Four THE BEAR STUDENTS

ACKNOWLEDGMENTS

As always, Barbara Zafft and Beverly Whitman of the Yellowstone Park Reference Library were of great help in locating obscure items.

Lee Whittlesey, Yellowstone bibliographer extraordinaire, reminded me of interesting historical bear material I had forgotten and told me about other material I had never even heard of.

Jim Peaco, Yellowstone photo-archivist, was of great help with historical photographs.

I must also thank Don Streubel, until recently director of the Yellowstone Institute. If he had not encouraged me to conduct a course for the institute in grizzly bear ecology and management, I might not have found the renewed interest in Yellowstone bear history that led eventually to this book.

The scientists who have studied Yellowstone's bears have given us all a great gift of knowledge. I dedicate this book to two friends, Steve and Marilynn French, whose studies of bear behavior in recent years have enriched that gift almost beyond imagining.

Last, I am grateful to many previous writers on Yellowstone, especially those devoted rangers who contributed so faithfully for so many years to *Yellowstone Nature Notes*. This book is in good part a testimonial to their affection for the bears of Yellowstone.

INTRODUCTION

It should have occurred to me long ago to do this book. In 1980, when the first edition of my book *The Bears of Yellowstone* was published, I felt disappointed that I had not been able to include in that volume more firsthand accounts of these remarkable and celebrated animals. I did devote about a third of the book to what might loosely be called cultural history, placing the bears in some greater social and historical context, but there was not room to let very many of the characters in the story speak in their own voices.

This book gives them that room. You can view it either as a companion volume for *The Bears of Yellowstone* or as a work that stands comfortably on its own. I have included a couple of accounts that appeared more or less completely in the previous book, but most have been lost to public attention since their first, and often quite obscure, appearance long ago.

Today the bears of Yellowstone are at the center of an apparently endless controversy, one that ignited in the 1960s and shows no sign of letting up. We Americans face great challenges in protecting these animals and their habitat. I and many others have written at length about those challenges, and a huge amount of scientific research has both illuminated and fueled the controversy.

Whenever I am out watching bears, however, all the ruckus, the political maneuvering, the overheated (and often slanted) journalism, and the generally panicky mood of today's bear management world fade a bit. I leave all that behind, and as I watch, the bears show me once again the wonder and beauty of their world.

I offer this book in that spirit. In our sense of urgency to do the right thing for these precious animals and their threatened environment, we can forget why we care so much in the first place. Though none of the dozens of accounts included in this book clearly tells you why, as you read you will begin to see the richness of Yellowstone bear lore and will yourself be reminded of why the battle over the bears has been so fiercely fought. In these little pieces of reminiscence and history, we can see how earlier generations struggled to come to terms with the fascination, amusement, fear, and sense of responsibility that the bears of Yellowstone still inspire today. Within each section of the book, the selections are arranged chronologically, and sometimes you can even see how attitudes evolved from decade to decade. A minimum of editing has been done to remove outdated scientific nomenclature and correct other obvious minor editorial problems.

As with any collection of this sort, drawn from a body of material as huge as the literature of Yellowstone, there is a certain amount of arbitrary selection and limitation. I've picked the material that seemed to best represent a cross-section of viewpoints and experiences, but I encourage you to search out more. The bears of Yellowstone have generated, and continue to generate, lots of stories, articles, and other miscellaneous published observations.

For the sake of controlling the book's scope, I have more or less restricted it to that era prior to the initiation of major scientific research work on Yellowstone bears, though it concludes with a few passages from Olaus Murie's pathbreaking 1943 study. If you want to learn more about today's bears, I especially recommend the publications of the various research teams who have worked in Yellowstone since 1943: the Craighead grizzly bear study and the Barnes and Bray black bear study of the 1960s, the various National Park Service reports since 1970, the Interagency Grizzly Bear Study that has been underway since 1973, and the Yellowstone Grizzly Foundation research that began in 1983.

But for now, turn the page and embark with a diverse and often bewildered company of travelers who found their way to Yellowstone back when our great adventure with the bears of the park had just begun.

Paul Schullery
Yellowstone
Winter 1990

Part One

THE EARLY NATURALISTS

————◆•◆•◆————

At the time of Yellowstone Park's establishment, in 1872, little was known of the natural history of bears, and much of what was known was either incorrect or at least confused. Bears had not attracted the serious attention of many scientists and were still generally treated as varmints.

Yellowstone would have a tremendous effect on public attitudes toward bears over the next few decades, as people from all over the country were able to watch bears with relatively little risk and to come to appreciate their fascinating qualities. A few early administrators and visitors attempted to analyze at least some aspects of Yellowstone bear life, long before these animals became one of the most studied of all American wildlife populations. These pioneers of Yellowstone bear study didn't always get the story right, but they made a start for us.

1880

Park Bears
Philetus Norris

Philetus Norris was the second superintendent of Yellowstone, serving in that capacity from 1877 to 1882. He was a colorful character, something of an adventurer, and one of the park's most energetic early defenders.

His account of the park's bears is longer on energy than on accuracy, but it reflects the soft, muddled manner of much informal nature writing at that time. Of course, only two species of bears live in Yellowstone, not six; his ascribing of distinct personality traits to these "varieties" of bears must have been at least in part the result of an overactive imagination. Still, Norris deserves considerable credit for at least going out and looking. In his day, his observations were not without merit, and he obviously devoted a good bit of time to watching bears.

The mountain men of this region believe that in the Park there are at least six varieties of the bear tribe, besides the long-tailed mud bear, or wolverine.

Grizzly bear. —The hog-back, or real California grizzly, with a mane upon the shoulders, is one of the largest, most powerful, ferocious, and dangerous animals upon the continent, but is less numerous than some other varieties within the Park. Specimens often occur of incredible size. At times one is met with which, when erect on its haunches—the customary position when looking for an enemy—will overtop in height a man on horseback. With one blow of its fearful fore paw and claws this animal is able to disembowel and kill any other animal of this region. One which I shot near Beaver Lake in the fall of 1879, after he had killed a valuable horse, was certainly heavier than any one of the more than fifty horses in our band. From his carcass thirty-five gallons of oil were obtained, and his skin, now in Washington, after being trimmed and dressed is still 8 feet 6 inches long (exclusive of the tail) and 6 feet 6 inches wide. Though but few larger than this have been taken, many but little inferior in size have been killed by different members of our parties. They seldom fail to cover with decaying logs, rubbish, or stones an elk or other animal they may kill, remaining near the body or returning nightly to it, as though a tempting dessert to their meal of grasshoppers, roots, and berries; for, human-like, they enjoy a mixed diet, though not so dainty as man in regard to its kind or quality. Although, save in defense of these carcasses or of its young, this bear seldom provokes attack upon man, it invariably resists one, and if wounded usually charges furiously, either to its own death or that of its foe, and not infrequently both. Indeed, it may truly be said to be the mountaineer's most dreaded foe.

Silver-tipped bear. —This animal is nearly destitute of a mane, and is somewhat smaller, less powerful and ferocious than the true grizzly; moreover its coat of hair is much longer than the latter's, and is tipped at the ends with a glistening, silvery white; hence the name.

Cinnamon bear. —This is so called from its reddish-brown color. It is somewhat longer and more slender than the smut-faced bear, and nearly his equal in audacious ferocity.

Smut-faced bear. —This is a still smaller animal, with a brockled, impish-looking face—a true indicator of the character of the beast. It is the most meddlesome and pugnacious of the bear family.

Black bear. —This animal in the Park only differs from those of the East in his greater size and the greater length and fineness of his fur, and is as elsewhere, either wild or domesticated, uniformly a less ferocious animal than any of the above-described species.

"Silk bear." —This provincialism is the only designation I have heard applied to this smallest and rarest variety of the bear family. The few of which I have personal knowledge were found near the upper limit

of timber, engaged in biting, in order to more easily break off for food, the cone-laden boughs of the piñon pines. They were all very fat, and had a coat of glistening black fur, fine and of extra length, rendering them more valuable than any of the species of the bear family.

All of these short-tailed varieties of bear hibernate in hollow trees, in eaves, or more frequently in rude wickeups, amid the dense evergreen declivities of the mountains, to which they retire early in winter, and remain until the accumulated snows thaw in spring, when they scramble out, often very lean, and always tender-footed, but soon recruit strength by devouring roots and mountain moles at the nearest slopes clear of snow. Few mountain scenes are more ludicrously interesting than that of half a dozen bears, of assorted colors and sizes, engaged in the sport of catching the burrowing mole just below some melting snow-drift upon the steep and slippery mountain side. In ignorance of their mode of making details for duty, I can only say that it seems to be the especial task of one of each party to pull up the sage-brush, thereby unearthing the moles; the rest of them, in their efforts to catch and eat them, often falling pell-mell over each other, like Chippewa Indians engaged in a game of Lacrosse. A variation of this sport is occasionally caused by a shower of explosive bullets from the repeating rifle of a grim mountaineer, perched unseen upon some overlooking snow-field, cliff, or tree-top.

1899

Death Gulch
T. A. Jaggar

There are a number of places in Yellowstone Park where hot springs, formed in small depressions or otherwise windless spots, have the power to kill small birds and mammals. In most of these it seems that death is not the result of some toxic gas, but instead is caused by suffocation: many springs give off carbon dioxide, and birds and mammals that wander into the spring's stagnant natural bowl are quickly overcome, possibly because their high respiration rates leave them no time to escape.

Death Gulch, as Jaggar explained, was another matter, at least as far as its power. Larger animals, wandering that way, were overcome, and their rotting carcasses attracted scavengers, including grizzly bears.

The gulch seems to have lost much of its power. Nearly thirty years of radiotelemetry of dozens of grizzly bears has not yet revealed even one that died there.

Cases of asphyxiation by gas have been very frequently reported of late years, and we commonly associate with such reports the idea of a second-rate hotel and an unsophisticated countryman who blows out the gas. Such incidents we connect with the supercivilization of the nineteenth century, but it is none the less true that Nature furnishes similar accidents, and that in regions far remote from the haunts of men. In the heart of the Rocky Mountains of Wyoming, unknown to either the tourist or the trapper, there is a natural hostelry for the wild inhabitants of the forest, where, with food, drink, and shelter all in sight, the poor creatures are tempted one after another into a bath of invisible poisonous vapor, where they sink down to add their bones to the fossil records of an interminable list of similar tragedies, dating back to a period long preceding the records of human history.

It was the writer's privilege, as a member of the expedition of the United States Geological Survey of the Yellowstone Park, under the direction of Mr. Arnold Hague, to visit and for the first time to photograph this remarkable locality. A similar visit was last made by members of the survey in the summer of 1888, and an account of the discovery of Death Gulch was published in Science (February 15, 1889) under the title A Deadly Gas Spring in the Yellowstone Park, by Mr. Walter Harvey Weed. The following extracts from Mr. Weed's paper indicate concisely the general character of the gulch, and the description of the death-trap as it then appeared offers interesting material for comparison with its condition as observed in the summer of 1897.

Death Gulch is a small and gloomy ravine in the northeast corner of the Yellowstone National Park. "In this region the lavas which fill the ancient basin of the park rest upon the flanks of mountains formed of fragmentary volcanic ejecta, . . . while the hydrothermal forces of the central portion of the park show but feeble manifestations of their energy in the almost extinct hot-spring areas of Soda Butte, Lamar River, Cache Creek, and Miller Creek." Although hot water no longer flows from these vents, "gaseous emanations are now given off in considerable volume." On Cache Creek, about two miles above its confluence with Lamar River, are deposits of altered and crystalline travertine, with pools in the creek violently effervescing locally. This is due to the copious emission of gas. Above these deposits "the creek cuts into a bank of sulphur and gravel cemented by this material, and a few yards beyond is the *débouchure* of a small lateral gully coming down from the mountain side. In its bottom is a small stream of clear and cold water, sour with sulphuric acid, and flowing down a narrow and steep channel cut in beds of dark-gray volcanic tuff. Ascending this gulch, the sides, closing together, become very steep slopes of white, decomposed rock. . . . The only springs now flowing are small oozes of water issuing from the base of these slopes, or from the channel bed, forming a thick, creamy, white deposit about the vents, and covering the stream bed. This deposit consists largely of sulphate of alumina. . . . About one hundred and fifty feet above the main stream these oozing springs of acid water cease, but the character of the gulch remains the same. The odor of sulphur now becomes stronger, though producing no other effect than a slight irritation of the lungs.

"The gulch ends, or rather begins, in a scoop or basin about two hundred and fifty feet above Cache Creek, and just below this was found the fresh body of a large bear, a silver-tip grizzly, with the remains of a companion in an advanced stage of decomposition above him. Near by were the skeletons of four more bears, with the bones of an elk a yard or two above, while in the bottom of the pocket were the fresh remains of several squirrels, rock hares, and other small animals, besides numerous dead butterflies and insects. The body of the grizzly was carefully examined for bullet holes or other marks of injury, but showed no traces of violence, the only indication being a few drops of blood under the nose. It was evident that he had met his death but a short time before, as the carcass was still perfectly fresh, though offensive enough at the time of a later visit. The remains of a cinnamon bear just above and alongside of this were in an advanced state of decomposition, while the other skeletons were almost denuded of flesh, though the claws and much of the hair remained. It was apparent that these animals, as well as the squirrels and insects, had not met their death by violence, but had been asphyxiated by the irrespirable gas given off in the gulch. The hollows were tested for carbonic-acid gas with lighted tapers without proving its presence, but the strong smell of sulphur, and a choking sensation of the lungs, indicated the presence of noxious gases, while the strong wind prevailing at the time, together with the open nature of the ravine, must have caused a rapid diffusion of the vapors.

"This place differs, therefore, very materially from the famous Death Valley of Java and similar places, in being simply a V-shaped trench, not over seventy-five feet deep, cut in the mountain slope, and not a hollow or cave. That the gas at times accumulates in the pocket at the head of the gulch is, however, proved by the dead squirrels, etc., found on its bottom. It is not probable, however,

Death Gulch as it appeared in 1897, when it was potent enough to kill bears regularly. Photo from Appleton's Popular Science Monthly, *February 1899.*

that the gas ever accumulates here to a considerable depth, owing to the open nature of the place, and the fact that the gulch draining it would carry off the gas, which would, from its density, tend to flow down the ravine. This offers an explanation of the death of the bears, whose remains occur not in this basin, but where it narrows to form the ravine, for it is here that the layer of gas would be deepest, and has proved sufficient to suffocate the first bear, who was probably attracted by the remains of the elk, or perhaps of the smaller victims of the invisible gas; and he, in turn, has doubtless served as bait for others who have in turn succumbed. Though the gulch has doubtless served as a death-trap for a very long period of time, these skeletons and bodies must be the remains of only the most recent victims, for the ravine is so narrow and the fall so great that the channel must be cleared out every few years, if not annually. The change wrought by the water during a single rainstorm, which occurred in the interval between Mr. Weed's first and second visits, was so considerable that it seems probable that the floods of early spring, when the snows are melting under the hot sun of this region, must be powerful enough to wash everything down to the cone of *débris* at the mouth of the gulch." Mr. Arnold Hague, on the occasion of his visit, was more successful in obtaining evidence of the presence of carbonic-dioxide gas. He writes: "The day I went up the ravine I was able in two places to extinguish a long brown paper taper. The day I was there it was very calm, and where I made the test the water was trickling down a narrow gorge shut in by shelving rocks above."

It was at noon on the 22nd of July in the summer of 1897 that we made camp near the mouth of Cache Creek, about three miles southeast of the military post and mail station of Soda Butte. In company with Dr. Francis P. King I at once started up the creek, keeping the left bank, that we might not miss the gulch, which joins the valley of Cache Creek from the southern side. We had a toilsome climb through timber and over steep embankments, cut by the creek in a loose conglomerate, and after going about a mile and a half we noticed that some of these banks were stained with whitish and yellow deposits of alum and sulphur, indicating that we were nearing the old hot-spring district. Soon a caved-in cone of travertine was seen, with crystalline calcite and sulphur in the cavities, and the bed of the creek was more or less completely whitened by these deposits, while here and there could be seen along the banks oozing "paint-pots" of calcareous mud, in one case inky black, with deposits of vari-colored salts about its rim, and a steady ebullition of gas bubbles rising from the bottom. In other cases these pools were crystal clear, and always cold. The vegetation, which below had been dense close to the creek's bank, here became more scanty, especially on the southern side, where the bare rock was exposed and seen to be a volcanic breccia, much decomposed and stained with solfataric deposits. A mound of coarse *débris* seen just above on this side indicated the presence of a lateral ravine, which from its situation and character we decided was probably the gulch sought for. A strong odor of sulphureted hydrogen had been perceptible for some time, and when we entered the gully the fumes became oppressive, causing a heavy burning sensation in the throat and lungs. The ravine proved to be as described, a V-shaped trench cut in the volcanic rock, about fifty feet in depth, with very steep bare whitish slopes, narrowing to a stony rill bed that ascended steeply back into the mountain side.

Climbing through this trough, a frightfully weird and dismal place, utterly without life, and occupied by only a tiny streamlet and an appalling odor, we at length discovered some brown furry masses lying scattered about the floor of the ravine about a quarter of a mile from the point where we had left Cache Creek. Approaching cautiously, it became quickly evident that we had before us a large group of huge recumbent bears; the one nearest to us was lying with his nose between his paws, facing us, and so exactly like a huge dog asleep that it did not seem possible that it was the sleep of death. To make sure, I threw a pebble at the animal, striking him on the flank; the distended skin resounded like a drumhead, and the only response was a belch of poisonous gas that almost overwhelmed us. Closer examination showed that the animal was a young silver-tip grizzly; a few drops of thick, dark-red blood stained his nostrils and the ground beneath. There proved to be five other carcasses, all bears, in various stages of decay; careful search revealed oval areas of hair and bones that represented two other bears, making a total of eight carcasses in all. Seven were grizzlies, one was a cinnamon bear. One huge grizzly was so recent a victim that his tracks were still visible in the white, earthy slopes, leading down to the spot where he had met his death. In no case were any marks of violence seen, and there can be no question that death was occasioned by the gas. The wind was blowing directly up the ravine during our visit, and we failed to get any test for carbonic acid, though we exhausted all our matches in the effort, plunging the flames into hollows of the rill bed in various parts of its course; they invariably burned brightly, and showed not the slightest tendency to extinguish. The dilution of the gas in such a breeze would be inevitable, however; that the gas was present was attested by the peculiar oppression on the lungs that was felt during the entire period that we were in the gulch, and which only wore off gradually on our return to camp. I suffered from a slight headache in consequence for several hours.

There was no difference in the appearance of the portion of the gulch where the eight bears had met their end and the region above and below. A hundred yards or more up stream the solfataric deposits become less abundant, and the timber grows close to the brook; a short distance beyond this the gulch ends. No bodies were found above, and only bears were found in the locality described. It will be observed that Weed's experience differs in this respect from ours, and the appearance of the place was somewhat different: he found elk and small animals in addition to the bears, and describes the death-trap as occupying the mouth of the basin at the head of the gulch, above the point where the last springs of acid water cease. The rill observed by us has its source far above the animals; indeed, it trickles directly through the worm-eaten carcass of the cinnamon bear—a thought by no means comforting when we realized that the water supply for our camp was drawn from the creek only a short distance down the valley.

It is not impossible that there may be two or three of these gullies having similar properties. That we should have found only bears may perhaps be accounted for on the ground that the first victim for this season was a bear, and his carcass frightened away all animals except those of his own family. For an illustration of a process of accumulation of the bones of large vertebrates, with all the conditions present necessary for fossilization, no finer example can be found in the world than Death Gulch; year after year the snow slides and spring floods wash down this fresh supply of entrapped carcasses to be buried in the waste cones and alluvial bottoms of Cache Creek and Lamar River. Probably the stream-formed conglomerate that we noted as we ascended the creek is locally filled with these remains.

The gas is probably generated by the action of the acid water on the ancient limestones that here underlie the lavas at no great depth; outcrops of these limestones occur only a few miles away at the mouth of Soda Butte Creek. This gas must emanate from fissures in the rock just above the bears, and on still nights it may accumulate to a depth of two or three feet in the ravine, settling in a heavy, wavy stratum, and probably rolling slowly down the bed of the rill into the valley below.

1899

The Death of Wahb
Ernest Thompson Seton

Ernest Thompson Seton was perhaps the most popular nature writer in America in the early 1900s. He produced a great flood of books and articles, including the classic short animal novel *The Biography of a Grizzly*. The *Biography* has been more or less continuously in print since 1899 and has been made into a movie; I suspect it may be the best-selling American bear book of all time.

The hero in the *Biography* was a grizzly bear named Wahb. Orphaned as a cub, Wahb grew into a fearsome, huge old boar that terrorized ranchers near the park and retreated into the park periodically for more peaceful times. In this closing episode, Wahb, harried by a smaller bear known as the Roachback, left his traditional hunting grounds and sought his final peace at Death Gulch.

Today, this story may seem hopelessly sentimental and anthropomorphic, and Seton had his critics on these grounds even back then. But Wahb was the first truly famous Yellowstone bear—fictional or real—and his demise no doubt moistened the eyes of thousands of young readers.

The Roachback's life was one of continual vigilance, always ready to run, doubling and shifting to avoid the encounter that must mean instant death to him. Many a time from some hiding-place he watched the great Bear, and trembled lest the wind should betray him. Several times his very impudence saved him, and more than once he was nearly cornered in a box-cañon. Once he escaped only by climbing up a long crack in a cliff, which Wahb's huge frame could not have entered. But still, in a mad persistence, he kept on marking the trees farther into the range.

At last he scented and followed up the sulphur-bath. He did not understand it at all. It had no appeal to him, but hereabouts were the tracks of the owner. In a spirit of mischief the Roachback scratched dirt into the spring, and then seeing the rubbing-tree, he stood side-wise on the rocky ledge, and was thus able to put his mark fully five feet above that of Wahb. Then he nervously jumped down, and was running about, defiling the bath and keeping a sharp lookout, when he heard a noise in the woods below. Instantly he was all alert. The sound drew near, then the wind brought the sure proof, and the Roachback, in terror, turned and fled into the woods.

It was Wahb. He had been failing in health of late; his old pains were on him again, and, as well as his hind leg, had seized his right shoulder, where were still lodged two rifle-balls. He was feeling very ill, and crippled with pain. He came up the familiar bank at a jerky limp, and there caught the odor of the foe; then he saw the track in the mud—his eyes said the track of a *small* Bear, but his eyes were dim now, and his nose, his unerring nose, said, "This is the track of the huge invader." Then he noticed the tree with his sign on it, and there beyond doubt was the stranger's mark far above his own. His eyes and nose were agreed on this; and more, they told him that the foe was close at hand, might at any moment come.

Wahb was feeling ill and weak with pain. He was in no mood for a desperate fight. A battle against such odds would be madness now. So, without taking the treatment, he turned and swung along the bench away from the direction taken by the stranger—the first time since his cubhood that he had declined to fight.

That was a turning-point in Wahb's life. If he had followed up the stranger he would have found the miserable little craven trembling, cowering, in an agony of terror, behind a log in a natural trap, a walled-in glade only fifty yards away, and would surely have crushed him. Had he even taken the bath, his strength and courage would have been renewed, and if not, then at least in time he would have

The Roachback fled into the woods. From The Biography of a Grizzly.

met his foe, and his after life would have been different. But he had turned. This was the fork in the trail, but he had no means of knowing it.

He limped along, skirting the lower spurs of the Shoshones, and soon came on that horrid smell that he had known for years, but never followed up or understood. It was right in his road, and he traced it to a small, barren ravine that was strewn over with skeletons and dark objects, and Wahb, as he passed, smelled a smell of many different animals, and knew by its quality that they were lying dead in this treeless, grassless hollow. For there was a cleft in the rocks at the upper end, whence poured a deadly gas; invisible but heavy, it filled the little gulch like a brimming poison bowl, and at the lower end there was a steady overflow. But Wahb knew only that the air that poured from it as he passed made him dizzy and sleepy, and repelled him, so that he got quickly away from it and was glad once more to breathe the piny wind.

Once Wahb decided to retreat, it was all too easy to do so next time; and the result worked double disaster. For, since the big stranger was allowed possession of the sulphur-spring, Wahb felt that he would rather not go there. Sometimes when he came across the traces of his foe, a spurt of his old courage would come back. He would rumble that thunder-growl as of old, and go painfully lumbering along the trail to settle the thing right then and there. But he never overtook the mysterious giant, and his rheumatism, growing worse now that he was barred from the cure, soon made him daily less capable of either running or fighting.

Sometimes Wahb would sense his foe's approach when he was in a bad place for fighting, and, without really running, he would yield to a wish to be on a better footing, where he would have a fair chance. This better footing never led him nearer the enemy, for it is well known that the one awaiting has the advantage.

Some days Wahb felt so ill that it would have been madness to have staked everything on a fight, and when he felt well or a little better, the stranger seemed to keep away.

Wahb soon found that the stranger's track was most often on the Warhouse and the west slope of the Piney, the very best feeding-grounds. To avoid these when he did not feel equal to fighting was only natural, and as he was always in more or less pain now, it amounted to abandoning to the stranger the best part of the range.

Weeks went by. Wahb had meant to go back to his bath, but he never did. His pains grew worse; he was now crippled in his right shoulder as well as in his hind leg.

The long strain of waiting for the fight begot anxiety, that grew to be apprehension, which, with the sapping of his strength, was breaking down his courage, as it always must when courage is founded on muscular force. His daily care now was not to meet and fight the invader, but to avoid him till he felt better.

Thus that first little retreat grew into one long retreat. Wahb had to go farther and farther down the Piney to avoid an encounter. He was daily worse fed, and as the weeks went by was daily less able to crush a foe.

He was living and hiding at last on the Lower Piney—the very place where once his Mother had brought him with his little brothers. The life he led now was much like the one he had led after that dark day. Perhaps for the same reason. If he had had a family of his own all might have been different. As he limped along one morning, seeking among the barren aspen groves for a few roots, or the wormy partridge-berries that were too poor to interest the Squirrel and the Grouse, he heard a stone rattle down the western slope into the woods, and, a little later, on the wind was borne the dreaded taint. He waded through the ice-cold Piney,—once he would have leaped it,—and the chill water sent through and up each great hairy limb keen pains that seemed to reach his very life. He was retreating again—which way? There seemed but one way now—toward the new ranch-house.

But there were signs of stir about it long before he was near enough to be seen. His nose, his trustiest friend, said, "Turn, turn and seek the hills," and turn he did even at the risk of meeting there the dreadful foe. He limped painfully along the north bank of the Piney, keeping in the hollows and among the trees. He tried to climb a cliff that of old he had often bounded up at full speed. When halfway up his footing gave way, and down he rolled to the bottom. A long way round was now the only road, for onward he must go—on—on. But where? There seemed no choice now but to abandon the whole range to the terrible stranger.

And feeling, as far as a Bear can feel, that he is fallen, defeated, dethroned at last, that he is driven from his ancient range by a Bear too strong for him to face, he turned up the west fork, and the lot was drawn. The strength and speed were gone from his once mighty limbs; he took three times as long as he once would to mount each well-known ridge, and as he went he glanced backward from time to time to know if he were pursued. Away up the head of the little branch were the Shoshones, bleak, forbidding; no enemies were there, and the Park was beyond it all—on, on he must go. But as he climbed with shaky limbs, and short uncertain steps, the west wind brought the odor of Death Gulch, that fearful little valley where everything was dead, where the very air was deadly. It used to disgust him and drive him away, but now Wahb felt that it had a message for him; he was drawn by it. It was in his line of flight, and he hobbled slowly toward the place. He went nearer, nearer, until he stood upon the entering ledge. A Vulture that had descended to feed on one of the victims was slowly going to sleep on the untouched carcass. Wahb swung his great grizzled muzzle and his long white beard in the wind. The odor that he once had hated was attractive now. There was a strange biting quality in the air. His body craved it. For it seemed to numb his pain and it promised sleep, as it did that day when first he saw the place.

Far below him, to the right and to the left and on and on as far as the eye could reach, was the great kingdom that once had been his; where he had lived for years in the glory of his strength; where none had dared to meet him face to face. The whole earth could show no view more beautiful. But Wahb had no thought of its beauty; he only knew that it was a good land to live in; that it had been his, but that now it was gone, for his strength was gone, and he was flying to seek a place where he could rest and be at peace.

Away over the Shoshones, indeed, was the road to the Park, but it was far, far away, with a doubtful end to the long, doubtful journey. But why so far? Here in this little gulch was all he sought; here were peace and painless sleep. He knew it; for his nose, his never-erring nose, said, "*Here! here now!*"

He paused a moment at the gate, and as he stood the wind-borne fumes began their subtle work. Five were the faithful wardens of his life, and the best and trustiest of them all flung open wide the door he long had kept. A moment still Wahb stood in doubt. His lifelong guide was silent now, had given up his post. But another sense he felt within. The Angel of the Wild Things was standing there, beckoning, in the little vale. Wahb did not understand. He had no eyes to see the tear in the Angel's eyes, nor the pitying smile that was surely on his lips. He could not even see the Angel. But he *felt* him beckoning, beckoning.

He paused a moment at the gate. From The Biography of a Grizzly.

A rush of his ancient courage surged in the Grizzly's rugged breast. He turned aside into the little gulch. The deadly vapors entered in, filled his huge chest and tingled in his vast, heroic limbs as he calmly lay down on the rocky, herbless floor and as gently went to sleep, as he did that day in his Mother's arms by the Graybull, long ago.

1903

Bear Life in the Yellowstone
Theodore Roosevelt

Theodore Roosevelt wrote many excellent articles on bears – so many, in fact, and of such good sense, that I gathered them into a book, *American Bears: Selections from the Writings of Theodore Roosevelt* (1983). Roosevelt visited Yellowstone several times, and though he never spent any time studying the local bears, he applied his writing skills to the information he gathered while in the park. He wrote the following paragraphs as part of an extended account of his famous 1903 presidential visit to the park. One short paragraph, describing photographs accompanying the original publication of this account, has been deleted.

We see here that the line between natural history and human drama was by 1903 completely erased when it came to writing about the bears of Yellowstone. Roosevelt, an astute and respected naturalist, spent much of his time recounting early "tourist stories" about the bears and their antics in camps and other developed areas. But his concluding paragraph was a perfect statement of the challenge and opportunity that the bears of Yellowstone offer to science.

It was in the interior of the Park, at the hotels beside the lake, the falls, and the various geyser basins, that we would have seen the bears had the season been late enough; but unfortunately the bears were still for the most part hibernating. We saw two or three tracks, but the animals themselves had not yet begun to come about the hotels. Nor were the hotels open. No visitors had previously entered the Park in the winter or early spring, the scouts and other employees being the only ones who occasionally traverse it. I was sorry not to see the bears, for the effect of protection upon bear life in the Yellowstone has been one of the phenomena of natural history. Not only have they grown to realize that they are safe, but, being natural scavengers and foul feeders, they have come to recognize the garbage heaps of the hotels as their special sources of food supply. Throughout the summer months they come to all the hotels in numbers, usually appearing in the late afternoon or evening, and they have become as indifferent to the presence of men as the deer themselves— some of them very much more indifferent. They have now taken their place among the recognized sights of the Park, and the tourists are nearly as much interested in them as in the geysers. In mussing over the garbage heaps they sometimes get tin cans stuck on their paws, and the result is painful. Buffalo Jones and some of the other scouts in extreme cases rope the bear, tie him up, cut the tin can off his paw, and let him go again. It is not an easy feat, but the astonishing thing is that it should be performed at all.

It was amusing to read the proclamations addressed to the tourists by the Park management, in which they were solemnly warned that the bears were really wild animals, and that they must on no account be either fed or teased. It is curious to think that the descendants of the great grizzlies which were the dread of the early explorers and hunters should now be semi-domesticated creatures, boldly hanging around crowded hotels for the sake of what they can pick up, and quite harmless so long as any reasonable precaution is exercised. They are much safer, for instance, than any ordinary bull or stallion, or even ram, and, in fact, there is no danger from them at all unless they are encouraged to grow too familiar or are in some way molested. Of course among the thousands of tourists there is a percentage of fools; and when fools go out in the afternoon to look at the bears feeding they occasionally bring themselves into jeopardy by some senseless act. The black bears and the cubs of the bigger bears can readily be driven up trees, and some of the tourists occasionally do this. Most of the animals never think of resenting it; but now and

By the time of Roosevelt's visit, some park bears were well adjusted to their role as garbage disposals. National Park Service photo.

then one is run across which has its feelings ruffled by the performance. In the summer of 1902 the results proved disastrous to a too inquisitive tourist. He was travelling with his wife, and at one of the hotels they went out toward the garbage pile to see the bears feeding. The only bear in sight was a large she, which, as it turned out, was in a bad temper because another party of tourists a few minutes before had been chasing her cubs up a tree. The man left his wife and walked toward the bear to see how close he could get. When he was some distance off she charged him, whereupon he bolted back toward his wife. The bear overtook him, knocked him down and bit him severely. But the man's wife, without hesitation, attacked the bear with that thoroughly feminine weapon, an umbrella, and frightened her off. The man spent several weeks in the Park hospital before he recovered. Perhaps the following telegram sent by the manager of the Lake Hotel to Major Pitcher illustrates with sufficient clearness the mutual relations of the bears, the tourists, and the guardians of the public weal in the Park. The original was sent me by Major Pitcher. It runs:

"Lake. 7-27-'03. Major Pitcher, Yellowstone: As many as seventeen bears in an evening appear on my garbage dump. To-night eight or ten. Campers and people not of my hotel throw things at them to make them run away. I cannot, unless there personally, control this. Do you think you could detail a trooper to be there every evening from say six o'clock until dark and make people remain behind danger line laid out by Warden Jones? Otherwise I fear some accident. The arrest of one or two of these campers might help. My own guests do pretty well as they are told. James Barton Key. 9 A.M."

Major Pitcher issued the order as requested.

At times the bears get so bold that they take to making inroads on the kitchen. One completely terrorized a Chinese cook. It would drive him off and then feast upon whatever was left behind. When a bear begins to act in this way or to show surliness it is sometimes necessary to shoot it. Other bears are tamed until they will feed out of the hand, and will come at once if called. Not only have some of the soldiers and scouts tamed bears in this fashion, but occasionally a chambermaid or waiter girl at one of the hotels has thus developed a bear as a pet.

This whole episode of bear life in the Yellowstone is so extraordinary that it will be well worth while for any man who has the right powers and enough time, to make a complete study of the life and history of the Yellowstone bears. Indeed, nothing better could be done by some of our out-door faunal naturalists than to spend at least a year in the Yellowstone, and to study the life habits of all the wild creatures therein. A man able to do this, and to write down accurately and interestingly what he had seen, would make a contribution of permanent value to our nature literature.

1906

A Photographic Expedition
William Wright

The more I read about bears and modern bear research, the more I am impressed by the books of William Wright. In *Ben the Black Bear* and *The Grizzly Bear,* both published in 1910, Wright summarized many years of careful observation of western bears. It would be decades before any bear book approached these for reliability as natural history, and few have surpassed them for entertainment.

He spent years as a hunter and guide before he gave up hunting to engage in full-time study of bears. In the following selection, he explained the circumstances that led him to Yellowstone and to its bears. I will only add what may not be immediately apparent to the inexperienced reader: this was photographic pioneering of the boldest sort. Its risks cannot be overemphasized, as Wright himself learned.

A great many years ago my interest in natural history, which grew out of my interest in hunting, caused me to give a certain amount of attention to photography. Little by little, as I became more expert in this, I took to carrying a camera with me on my various expeditions, and finally I came to making excursions with no other end in view than the photographing of game. It was a long time, however, before I developed a definite ambition to photograph a grizzly, because the difficulties which presented themselves in that field were so many that at first I saw no way of overcoming them.

Much hunting has not only made the grizzly very shy, but has caused him gradually to become even more nocturnal or, to be accurate, crepuscular, than he was originally. It follows that in these latter days the chances of obtaining a daylight picture of a grizzly are almost negligible, and though by some lucky chance one might meet a bear in a snap-shotting light when one had a camera ready, the coincidence would be too unlikely to depend upon. When, therefore, I began to think seriously of attempting to photograph these bears, I of necessity turned my mind to flash-light, and for several years I worked and experimented to that end. The most favorable time to operate being between sundown and dark, it was impracticable to set up a camera and leave the lens open and provide for the exploding of a flash when the bear came along, and I therefore set about perfecting an electrical device which at the same time would explode the flash and spring the shutter of the camera. My first idea was to have this apparatus operated by the bear himself, and to that end I constructed it so that the trigger could be tripped by pressure applied to a fine thread or wire, which could be stretched across the trail; but though I soon succeeded in getting this mechanism to work well at home, actual practice in the field developed a succession of difficulties which had to be overcome little by little, and as field trials were scarce and expensive, it took me a long time to arrive at satisfactory results.

By the time my camera was in working order, the bears on which I had expected to use it were all but things of the past; and having heard for a number of years that the grizzlies of the Yellowstone National Park had become comparatively tame, and that it was no difficult task to photograph them, and having hunted grizzlies in all the country round the park without finding the bears there different from what they were in other parts of the country, I determined to take my camera to the park and study the grizzly in this field. This was in 1906.

I was armed with a permit from Major Pitcher, the acting superintendent, which allowed me to photograph and study the grizzlies, provided I did not molest them in any way. I went first to the Grand Cañon. I found there quite a number of grizzlies feeding in the evening at the garbage dump back of the hotel, and for a few evenings

William Wright, as pictured in his book Ben the Black Bear *(the cub is not from Yellowstone).*

I watched them there in order to determine the direction from which they came, and to ascertain how many were using this feeding ground. After watching for a few evenings I found that there were about thirty grizzlies all told that came there. There were several old she bears with litters of cubs, several litters two and three years old that had left their mothers, but were still running together, and several old fellows that came and went by themselves.

While I was watching the dump in the evening, I travelled the surrounding country by day to see if any of these bears could be seen by daylight, and though I scoured every thicket and gully, not a grizzly did I thus see during some two weeks' sojourn there. In this respect they were much more timid than they were in a great many places throughout the Selkirk and Rocky Mountain ranges.

My next move was to find out where these bears hid when they were not feeding, for I have never yet seen a grizzly that did not have a home, either in some dense thicket or in some heavy timber or in some high mountain. I followed some of the more travelled trails for several miles and found that nearly all of these grizzlies had their headquarters in the range of mountains around Mt. Washburn. I then selected their largest highway, and after setting up my camera, concealed myself one evening about a hundred feet from the trail and to leeward of it, and watched for the coming of the grizzlies. Across the trail I had stretched a number forty sewing thread, one end attached to the electric switch and the other to a small stake driven into the ground beyond the trail. Just below where I had located, there was an open park in which the bears had been feeding, as was shown by the grass that had been nipped and the holes that had been dug for roots.

For some hours I waited in the bushes and fought gnats and mosquitoes. I saw several black bears pass along the hillside, but not a grizzly showed his nose until after the sun had set and the little marsh in the park was covered with a mantle of fog. Suddenly then, far up the trail, appeared what at first looked like a shadow, so slowly and silently did it move. But I knew at once, by the motion of the head and the long stride, that a grizzly was coming to the bottom for a few roots and a feed of grass.

I watched closely to see if he acted differently from bears elsewhere that are supposed to know less of man. I could not, however, detect the slightest difference in his actions from those of bears that had never seen Yellowstone Park. All his movements were furtive and cautious, as if he expected to meet an enemy at every step. He would advance a few feet, and then stop, turn his head from side to side, scent the air, and peer in every direction.

I was, of course, very anxious to see what he would do when he came to the thread across the trail, and I had not long to wait, for he came on steadily but slowly and, when within ten feet of the thread, he stopped, poked out his nose and sniffed two or three times, raised up on his hind feet, took a few more sniffs, and then bolted up the trail in the direction from which he had come. This bear did not seem to have been very successfully tamed.

A few minutes after he had gone three more appeared. These were evidently of one litter and appeared to be between two and three years old. They came on with the same cautious movements, and when they were close upon the thread, they also stopped and went through a similar performance. The one in front pushed out his nose and sniffed gingerly at the suspicious object. Those in the rear also stopped, but being curious to learn what was causing the blockade, the second one placed his forefeet on the rump of the one in front, in order to see ahead, while the third one straightened up on his hind legs and looked over the other two. They made a beautiful group, and just as they had poised themselves, the one in front must have touched the string a little harder than he had intended to, for there was a sudden flash that lit up the surroundings, and I expected to see the bears go tearing off through the timber, but, to my utter surprise, nothing of the kind happened. They all three stood up on their hind legs, and looked at each other as much as to say, "Now, what do you think of that?" and then they took up their investigation where it had been interrupted, followed the thread to where it was fastened to the stick, clawed up the spool, which I had buried in the ground, sniffed at it, and then went back to the trail, where they had first found the thread. Here they again stood up, and then, having either satisfied their curiosity or becoming suspicious, they turned around and trailed away through the timber. As far as I could see them they went cautiously, and stopped at frequent intervals to stand up and look behind them to see if there were any more flashes or if anything was following them. Unfortunately this picture was utterly worthless. I had failed to use enough flash powder, and when I came to develop the plate, it showed only the dimmest outline of the animals.

Soon after this an old she bear with three cubs came down the trail, but they were just as cautious as the others had been. Every few feet the mother would stop and sniff the air, and the cubs, fascinating little imitators that they are, had to copy her every move. If she stood up on her hind feet, they also stood up on theirs. If she stopped to sniff the air, they would run up and, placing their tiny feet against her sides, would peer wisely and anxiously ahead, until the old lady started on again. When she came to the thread she stopped short, and while she was making her investigations the cubs stood with their forefeet against her and awaited the verdict. It was sudden and apparently surprising, for, after satisfying herself that the obstacle was placed there for no good, she gave a lively snort that could have been heard for a hundred yards, and without waiting for her youngsters to get down, suddenly turned tail and, upsetting the whole lot, disappeared up the trail like a whirlwind, with the cubs trying their best to overtake her.

After this last delegation had gone I waited for an hour or more, but got no more photographic opportunities. Several bears came out, but it was too dark for me to follow their actions, and none of them saw fit to run into the thread. However, just before I was about to leave, I heard something coming down the trail as if pursued by the devil, and it occurred to me that whatever it was would be in too much of a hurry to stop and examine the string, and so it proved. There was a bright flash, and for an instant the forest was lighted up, and I saw an old black bear travelling as if for dear life. I had thought that he was at his best gait before he struck the string, but in this I was mistaken. He had only been fooling along before. Now he got down to business, and in less time than it takes to write it he was out of sight and beyond hearing. When I developed the plate it looked as though a cannonball of hair had been shot across it.

This was my first evening, and it did not pan out very heavily in practical results. But I had had a lot of sport, and had begun to find out, as later on I was to prove more thoroughly, that the Yellowstone Park grizzlies differ in no material respect from others of their species.

The next afternoon at about two o'clock I was again in my place of observation, with everything again in readiness for business. This time, thinking that it might not be so easy to detect, I had substituted a tiny wire for the thread. The wire was the finest that I could buy, the kind that florists use for winding flowers, and unless I knew exactly where it was, I could not see it myself when ten feet away from it. I had now selected a spot where the trail wound around between some fallen trees, where there was little danger of the bears getting scent of the wire before they came immediately upon it.

About six o'clock there came up a heavy thunder-storm and for more than an hour it rained in torrents. When I saw the storm approaching, I walked over a little way from the trail, peeled the bark from a couple of small trees, and covered my camera and my can of batteries, to keep them from getting wet. The flash-pan was fitted with a loose cover, easily thrown off by the exploding powder, and having thus protected my apparatus, I put on my rain coat, crawled under a thick-limbed, umbrellalike tree, and waited for the storm to pass. In the middle of it I saw a small black bear coming through the timber and headed for my shelter. At every flash of lightning he would make a dash for the nearest tree, but by the time he reached it the flash would be over and he would come on again. Just as he got within fifty yards of me there came a tremendous bolt, and chained lightning seemed to run down every tree. This was followed, or rather accompanied, by a splitting crash of thunder, and the small bear made one jump into the nearest tree, and never stopped till he got near the top, where he crouched down on a limb, rolled himself into a little ball, with his nose between his feet, and never moved until the disturbance was over.

When the rain had passed, I returned to where I could watch the trail, and waited for the grizzlies. It was not long before I saw an old bear coming down the trail. He was very large and fat and would, I imagine, have weighed from six to seven hundred pounds, and when I saw him advancing with the usual precautionary tactics, I was well pleased that it had rained, for I imagined that the water must have obliterated all scent, and that this old fellow was sure to run against my wire. But I was mistaken. When some six feet away he stopped, nosed his way slowly up, and stood for some seconds only a few inches from it. Then he became interested and worked a little nearer, and then there was a flash and he immediately stood up on his hind feet, much startled, and looking first in one direction and then in another. Then, like the three bears of the evening before, he started an investigation. He dropped down on all-fours, started to follow the wire toward the switch, changed his mind, worked along till he came to the little stick, and finally dug up the spool that was buried there. After thoroughly examining this he returned to the trail and followed my tracks down to where I had taken the bark off the trees. Here he nosed about for some time, and then finally turned to the right and disappeared in the timber. This negative proved to be a fairly good one, but it was not quite what I had hoped to obtain, as the bear had stopped short at the flash, while I would have preferred him in motion.

I now put in a new fuse and rearranged the camera, and it was not long before an old she bear and two cubs came down the trail; but she, after the usual preliminary examination, proved suspicious of the arrangement, and after smelling carefully along the wire, turned to the right and passed around the machine. I had brought with me on this evening a hand camera of the reflex type, built expressly for natural-history work, and I had set up my apparatus near the edge of the open park, thinking that perhaps a bear might come out in time for me to get a snap-shot of him before dark. After the old bear and cubs had passed, I crawled very cautiously to the edge of this opening and waited for them there. It was really too dark for a picture, but I thought that I might at least have the satisfaction of making a try for one. I expected that, after circling the camera, they would come out into the marsh, and this they did; but instead of passing along it as I had looked to see them do, they turned and came across it straight toward me. I was standing with the camera before my face, watching in the mirror all that was going on, and, as I remained perfectly quiet, the animals did not see me until they were within fifty or sixty feet of me. Then they went up on their hind legs, with a cub standing on either side of the old bear, and as the camera clicked, the mother dropped down and scuttled away up the marsh. About fifty feet from where they had stood there was a large tree, and as the old bear passed around this she was, for an instant, out of sight, and the two cubs, that had just then turned to follow her, stood perfectly still and appeared to be thoroughly mystified. Apparently she missed them about the same moment. She jumped back, and poking her head around the tree, gave two quick, short, emphatic "whoofs," and the way those cubs dropped and flew to her was a caution. She waited until they reached her side, and then gave each one of them a sharp cuff that bowled it over, and then both mother and cubs disappeared in the gathering darkness. When I developed the plate it was not even fogged by the exposure.

For another hour or more I watched my set camera. The storm had now entirely passed and the moon was shining, so that it was quite light in the little glade outside the timber. I saw four more grizzlies, including the three that had come out the night before, but they all avoided the wire. On the following evening I again tried for flash-lights, and while I saw ten grizzlies, they acted in about the usual way. Not one of them set off the flash. Those that had already had experience with the apparatus did not come within a hundred yards of me, and even those that I had not seen before seemed suspicious. This night I saw an old she grizzly with four cubs, and although I have seen quite a number of black bears with that number, this was the second time that I had ever seen a grizzly with so many.

For three nights more I tried different places along the trails, but did not get another exposure. Some of them came and nosed about, but most of them turned off at quite a distance from the wire, and finally they abandoned this trail altogether, and made use of two others that ran through the timber at quite a distance from it. Finding, therefore, that the bears at the cañon had evidently taken alarm at my operations, I determined to move over to the lake, sixteen miles away, as there were also said to be many grizzlies at that point.

Here, as at the cañon, I watched the garbage pile for two or three evenings, and scoured the country thereabout during the day. Finally I decided on a trail that led out of the range of thickly timbered hills, down through some heavy woods and underbrush toward the west. Here, also, I selected a spot for my camera at the edge of a little open glade, that was covered with grass and small willows. Through this glade the main trail ran, and a branch trail also wound around at its edge near the timber. I chose the through trail for my work, because its being nearly covered with grass afforded me a longed-for opportunity to conceal the wire. I also avoided setting my camera on the ground, and fastened it to an iron spike made for that purpose, and driven into the trunk of a large tree about twenty-five feet from the path. The flash-pan was set near the same tree, and the whole effectually concealed by means of cut willow branches stuck upright in the ground. The wire from the switch was led through the long grass about a foot from the ground, and its further end tied to a small willow.

When things were thus fixed to my liking, I myself retired to a spot from which I could see some two hundred yards up the trail, and get an unobstructed view of the glade itself, and I took care to finish these arrangements early enough in the evening to give the man scent a chance to dissipate before the grizzlies came out. I found, however, that there were so many black bears in this neighborhood that I was frequently obliged to show myself in order to frighten them from the trail, and protect my apparatus from their mischievous curiosity.

The first grizzly came down the trail about sundown. He acted much as those at the cañon had, and like them, he detected the wire before he touched it. He nosed along it inquisitively, and then in a rash moment tried to claw it, when, of course, there was a flash, and he actually turned a complete somersault and disappeared up the trail at such speed that, as I discovered the next day, he fairly tore up the earth as he went.

Somewhat to my surprise my next visitors proved to be the three grizzlies that had sprung my flash at the cañon. I recognized them easily by the markings on the shoulder and neck of one of them. I may say here in passing, if it surprises any one to speak of recognizing a bear previously encountered, that there is to the full as much individuality in bears as in people, and that it is perfectly easy for me to recognize a grizzly once seen and closely examined, and under such circumstances as I am here describing I could tell a newcomer the moment he came into sight on the trail.

These three bears came up to the spot where the wire was stretched, took one good sniff, and appearing to recognize it as the same outfit with which they already had had experience, turned unconcernedly to their right and passed by on the other side.

Just before dark a she grizzly and two cubs made their appearance, but just as they arrived at the fork of the trail they stopped, stood up, sniffed anxiously at the air, and then dropped down and sidled off, with uneasy backward glances, as though they not only suspected something wrong, but feared that it might pursue them. This old bear was unusually light in color, appearing indeed, in that light, almost silvery white over her entire body, while both her cubs, from where I stood, appeared to be almost jet black. After this I waited until it was so dark that I could not see a bear in the timber, and having obtained no more shots, I returned to camp.

All this time I had been struggling against a number of difficulties, photographic and electrical. Chief among the latter was the fuse for my flash-pan. I had found no difficulty in this regard when using a shutter exposure as slow as one-quarter of a second; but if, as was apt to be the case, there was any daylight remaining, this exposure was too slow and recorded movement on the part of the animal. I had, however, succeeded in finding an extremely fine imported German-silver wire, which fused rapidly enough to allow me to use the shutter exposure of a hundredth second.

My first supply of this wire having been limited, I had ordered more, and discovered, when too late, that it was of a slightly different size; and hence, to my chagrin, when I came to develop the three exposures which I succeeded in getting, I found that my shutter had worked too rapidly for the fuse, and my places showed no trace of an image.

At the time, however, I thought that I was getting along satisfactorily, and the next evening I again set up my camera at the same place. It now occurred to me that it might be possible, by reversing my former tactics and leaving my scent liberally scattered over the neighborhood, to allay the suspicions of these bears who were reputed to be accustomed to the presence of man. I therefore walked up and down the trail for some hundreds of feet and again concealed myself where I could watch without being seen.

The first bear delegation numbered three, but they were not my friends of the cañon, being, for one thing, considerably larger. I judged them to be nearly three years old, and they would have weighed, I should say, in the neighborhood of three hundred pounds apiece. They were as sleek as seals, and one of them had a beautiful silver coat. When they reached the point to which I had walked up the trail, they stopped and scented for a few moments, turned their heads in the direction in which I had gone, and then came on, paying no further attention to the matter. This encouraged me, and I began to think that my ruse was to prove successful; but when he reached the wire the leader stopped abruptly, and the three then stood up, looked at each other knowingly, and then, for all the world as though they inferred a connection between my scent and the presence of the wire, began methodically to track me up.

I was standing near a tree, and, not having expected any such move on their part, I had not taken the precaution to step back out of sight, and now I did not dare to move for fear of frightening them. I therefore stood absolutely still and watched their play with close attention and absorbed interest. They followed my every turn as unerringly as a hound follows a hare, and came on withal as silently as three shadows. Of course I had been careful to select a station to leeward of the trail, and this now helped to postpone their discovery of me. When within fifty feet of me they came to a fallen log, and, when the leader had his front paws on this, he stopped and looked ahead as though he felt that he was nearing that which he sought. The second bear started to pass him, but he turned his head and very gently took his companion by the nose with his mouth, whereupon he also stopped, and they both looked straight at me. However, as I did not move a muscle, they seemed unable to make out whether I was a living object or an inanimate one, and they again moved cautiously forward, still in absolute silence. When about twenty-five feet away, they again stood up and examined me intently, evidently doubting whether I were a bona-fide stump. Here, indeed, would have been a glorious opportunity, had I had a camera in hand, and had there been a trifle more light.

But they had come as far as they cared to. Dropping silently on to all-fours, they suddenly abandoned their investigations and bolted, only to stop at the end of a hundred feet, stand up again, again approach within fifty feet or so of me, and then turn aside and trail away through the trees. Soon after this, three more grizzlies came down to the forks of the trail. These were a trifle smaller than the others, but by far the handsomest that I had seen. Two of them were rather dark, while the third was a fine-looking animal, with a snow-white head, and silvery as far back as his shoulders. This is a typical marking, but in this case it was strangely accentuated, in spite of which, however, his companions seemed to approve of him since they had intrusted him with the leadership.

Like the others, they stopped at the string and, still like the others, they then took up my trail and that of the first three bears, and followed it as surely and as silently as the others had done. This time I took the precaution to keep behind the tree, and these three bears actually came up within ten feet of me before they discovered my presence. Then, up they went on their hind feet, and for a second there was another great picture before me: their thick, furry coats were magnificent, and the long hair standing out stiffly under their jaws lent a curious expression to their faces.

But, the second over, they too, after retreating and advancing once or twice, made their way silently into the forest.

After some waiting, an old she bear with two yearling cubs came along, apparently in a hurry, and acting as though they were late for an engagement. I thought for a moment that they were going through without stopping, but just as she reached the wire, the mother stopped short, took a hurried sniff, and then, apparently thinking it of no consequence, hurried on again. She changed her mind, however, almost instantly, but although the three turned tail and reared up on their hind legs, instead of running away, they appeared to be more curious than frightened; and it was only after rather a thorough examination of the wire and its surroundings, that they retreated up the trail, lingeringly, and with repeated glances over their shoulders.

I had hardly reset my apparatus when an old fellow came along, so huge of frame that, had he been in good condition instead of gaunt and famished looking, he would have weighed eight hundred pounds. But he looked as if he had not had a square meal all summer. His neck was long, his body thin, his legs ungainly, but still showing the tremendous muscles typical of the species. He seemed to take four-foot strides, and I thought that surely so great a brute would not stop to bother over a little wire; but, on the contrary, he not only stopped, but nosed his way carefully along until he came to the flash-pan. This was placed upon a pole, and was about six feet above the ground, and the old bear stood up on his hind legs and looked into it, after which he followed the battery wires to the camera, and then, returning, stood up a second time and stuck his nose into the flash-pan. I am afraid that if I had had a finger on the wire that controlled the switch, the temptation to pull it would have been too much for me. Meanwhile the bear, having again examined the camera, deliberately turned back and disappeared up the trail, and, much to my surprise, I saw no more of him.

My next visitor was the largest grizzly that I had yet seen. He would, I should judge, have weighed close to a thousand pounds, and he was at once so old and so fat that it was laughable to see him walk. He was rather dark in color, his back looked as if it were two feet broad and perfectly flat, and his legs did not seem to be more than a foot long. His ears were hardly visible. Perhaps he had lost most of them in the riots and ructions of a long-vanished youth. Hope dies hard, even at the hand of experience, and I again flattered myself that this old veteran would not pay any attention to my petty schemes. He came to the forks of the trail and—took the other turning. Then, appearing to change his mind, he turned back and came down my trail; and, accepting this as an omen, I counted a picture of him, broadside on, as already secured. But when he reached the wire, he not only stopped and sniffed at it for several seconds, but then reared up on his hind feet, gave a snort that could have been heard for a hundred yards, and then whirled about like a demoralized coward, and tried to run. Even in my disappointment I could not help laughing at the ludicrous spectacle. I am sure that he touched the ground in at least five places at every jump, and he seemed to think that he was going along at a tremendous gait, whereas, in reality, he was making the slowest kind of time. And he was so frightened that he had no time to look where he was going; he smashed into pretty much everything he came to, and for five minutes I could hear the breaking of brush and dead branches as he crashed through the timber.

Just as I was about to pack up for the night, I heard a commotion down the trail, and looking up I saw the three bears that I had first met at the cañon coming toward me in full flight. They had evidently taken some other path to the feeding ground, and, something having frightened them, they were now coming back my way at their best gait, and quite oblivious of the wire, into which they ran with such force that it parted. This time, however, they did not stop to investigate the result, but acted as though they felt the devil himself was after them, and disappeared up the trail, at what I think must be about the limit of a grizzly's speed.

Compare the bulk of the bear with that of the man; it was easy enough to overestimate the weight of a bear under these circumstances.

I had to leave in the morning for a trip to the Pacific Coast, and now gathered up my outfit and started for camp, supposing that my adventures were at an end.

In a knapsack on my back I had my tripod and flash-pan, the switchboard, and the connecting wires. In one hand I carried my camera, while in the other I had a covered sheet-iron box containing six dry batteries, the while being securely tied with a small rope. I intended, on my way to camp, to see the agent of the transportation company, and arrange for a set on an outgoing coach for the next morning; and to this end I approached the rear of a small mess house belonging to the transportation company, situated behind and on one side of the hotel. Now it happened that back of this mess house two barrels of refuse had been left standing. This was contrary to the regulations of the park, and Major Pitcher, the acting superintendent, told me afterward that all the trouble they have ever had with grizzlies arose from breaches of this rule. However, knowing nothing of this at the time, I was walking along without making any noise, and when directly back of the building, and not more than fifty feet away from it, I heard a sudden rattling among the cans, and out shot two grizzlies, followed, at a distance of about twenty feet, by a larger one. Taking it for granted that they saw me, and having, under such circumstances, no fear of the animals, I kept straight on, and thus, after a few steps, interposed myself between the last bear and the barrel from which he had been feeding. This he seemed to resent, for he turned angrily and started toward me. The whole situation developed, and indeed concluded, suddenly, so that I had no time for conscious planning. As the bear turned toward me I stopped rather mechanically, thinking that he, too, would stop before he came up to me; for I had never, in all my experience, had a bear attack me, and had always maintained that no grizzly would attack a man except under peculiar circumstances. However, this bear was either an exception to my rule, or else he considered the circumstances "peculiar."

It did not take him long to reach me, and, as he did so, he rose up and struck at my ribs with his right paw. The only weapon at hand being my can of batteries, and this, weighing about twenty pounds, being no mean defence if handled rightly, I swung it at him, hoping to stop him with the blow. As I did so, however, I advanced my left hand, and the bear's paw caught my camera, ripping out the front board and the magnet and wires attached to it. Almost at the same time I landed somewhere with the can, and, although the stroke did him no damage, it did set him back a foot or two, and turned what had doubtless been nothing but ill-temper into rage. With a loud snort he came at me again, and this time he raised himself to his full height and aimed a vicious stroke at my head; and I, seeing what was coming, ducked and closed in on him. And I was just in time, for I felt the wind from the blow, and his paw tore my hat from my head, and then, passing down the side of my face, struck me a glancing blow on the shoulder. Nothing, I think, but my nearness to the bear saved my life. Meanwhile, as I had ducked and closed in, I had swung my right hand back of me, and just as the bear delivered his blow at me, I landed mine on him; and as I had swung my can of batteries in a half-circle over my head, they came down with tremendous force.

I must have caught him somewhere about the head, for it felt as though I had struck a board, and the bear went over backward with an astonished bawl, and when he regained his feet, he was tail toward me and kept this position as long as I could see him. The first jump he made landed him head on against a dry-goods box; at the next he smashed into a tree; but he finally got his bearings and made off, if anything, faster than he had come at me.

When I had got my bearings, I looked around for my hat, but, being unable to find it in the half light, decided to hunt it up in the morning. I was not, at the moment, conscious of very great excitement, but when I reached camp I found that my hands were trembling rather uncomfortably, and it was several days before I recovered my usual absence of nerves. The next day, when I rescued my hat, I found two holes in the soft brim through which the bear had driven his claws, and one corner of my iron battery case was broken open like a ship's bow after a collision.

I am quite satisfied that had I made any noise as I approached the place where the bears had been feeding, they would have retreated before I reached them; but the ground was soft and my steps were noiseless. And, hungry as they doubtless were, one of them resented my sudden interruption of their feast.

Altogether I did not find the grizzlies of Yellowstone Park in any degree more tame or less cunning than they are to-day, for example, in the Selkirks. Many of them, it is true, come to the garbage piles to feed, but these very bears, fifty yards back in the timber, are again as wild as any of them anywhere. I was both surprised and interested by this, and, after watching them carefully from the positions provided for the public, I repeatedly concealed myself and watched them from the woods back of these feeding grounds. I can think of no better way to describe their actions and their attitudes than to liken them to the actions and attitudes of a man about to dive into the water. At the cañon, the garbage pile is in a hollow at the foot of rather a steep incline that leads up to the edge of the woods. Bear after bear coming down the trails that converge toward this point will stop as he reaches the brink of this declivity, glance downward, turn his head from side to side, and launch himself downhill, with the same air of committing himself to a foreign element that one sees in the upward glance and deep breath of a man launching himself from a diving-board. On their return, they invariably halted for a few seconds at the top of the hill, looked around, occasionally shook themselves, and with their first step up the familiar trail, resumed every sign of their habitual caution and alertness. While on the garbage pile itself they appear to pay scant attention to the people gathered behind the fairly distant wire fence, but even there, an eye familiar with their actions would note the constant watch they kept on what was going on and the hurried way in which they fed; and, fifty feet from the edge of the surrounding timber, they would, at the least scent or sound or sight, bolt as incontinently as in the farthest hills. Grizzlies are no more plentiful around the park to-day than they were twenty-five years ago in the Bitter Roots, and a hundred yards from the garbage pile they are no different.

Part Two

BEAR VERSUS MAN

Though most bear-human encounters in Yellowstone have been peaceful, the potential for violence has added a complicated element to our image of park bears. While we have been encouraged, by countless cartoon characters, children's stories, and commercial symbols, to think of bears as something other than wild animals, the bears of Yellowstone have occasionally reminded us of that potential.

It seems amazing to me that it took such a short time from the establishment of the park to the day when even experienced bear authorities considered Yellowstone's bears harmless. Bears have a complex image in most cultures; their ability to stand upright, their skilful exploitation of a great variety of foods and habitats, and their general appeal as roly-poly, warm fuzzy creatures have all tended to make humans consider them something more than wild animals—something more nearly human. Here in Yellowstone, that complex image has regularly been reinforced by violent encounters between bears and people.

1870

The Bear that Got Away
Walter Trumbull

Ever since the rise of the "Big-bear" school of tall tales in the American South-east before the Civil War, humor has been an important part of bear stories. This little tale came from Walter Trumbull, a member of the 1870 Washburn-Langford-Doane expedition to explore the Yellowstone area. In it, Trumbull poked fun at himself and his overarmed colleagues for their behavior while tracking a sow grizzly bear and her two cubs.

I have chosen, in this volume, to print these accounts "warts and all," which in this case means that Trumbull's racist terminology ("as the darkie said . . .") appears in its original form. This was another time, and it was not without its troubles and failings, any more than ours is.

Some of the party who had gone a short distance ahead to find out the best course to take the next day, soon returned and reported a grizzly and her two cubs about a quarter of a mile from camp. Six of the party decorated themselves as walking armories, and at once started in pursuit. Each individual was sandwiched between two revolvers and a knife, was supported around the middle by a belt of cartridges, and carried in his hand a needle carbine. Each one was particularly anxious to be the first to catch the bear, and an exciting foot-race ensued until the party got within 300 yards of the place

47

where the bear was supposed to be concealed. The foremost man then suddenly got out of breath, and, in fact, they all got out of breath. It was an epidemic. A halt was made, and the brute loudly dared to come out and show itself, while a spirited discussion took place as to what was best to do with the cubs. The location was a mountain side, thickly timbered with tall straight pines having no limbs within thirty feet of the ground. It was decided to advance more cautiously to avoid frightening the animal, and every tree which there was any chance of climbing was watched with religious care, in order to intercept her should she attempt to take refuge in its branches. An hour was passed in vain search for the sneaking beast, which had evidently taken to flight. Then this formidable war party returned to camp, having a big disgust at the cowardly conduct of the bear, but, as the darkie said, "not having it bad." Just before getting in sight of camp, the six invincibles discharged their firearms simultaneously, in order to show those remaining behind just how they would have slaughtered the bear, but more particularly just how they did not. This was called the "Bear Camp."

1877

A Washburn Grizzly Hunt
William Pickett

Sport hunting was legal in Yellowstone Park until 1883, when most park wild-life came under protection through a no-hunting regulation. There were few facilities in the park, and a certain amount of hunting was often necessary unless you carried all your food with you on the slow and still arduous trip to the park's attractions.

William Pickett, a former Confederate colonel and later a prominent sportsman and conservationist, was new to the west when he made this hunt. He later became famous for his ability to kill grizzly bears, but on this hunt he seems to have done almost everything wrong, wasting even the trophy to be had by taking the skin.

By mid-September, many of Yellowstone's bears have shifted into a sort of metabolic overdrive, consuming huge quantities of food in preparation for winter denning. This bear was probably up on Mount Washburn for whitebark pine nuts or to pick off the occasional bull elk that gets careless and inattentive to self-preservation during the fall rut.

Pickett occupies an interesting little niche in Yellowstone bear history. He was the one nonfictional character in Seton's *Biography of a Grizzly*. In that book, Pickett was the mean old rancher who orphaned the cub Wahb by shooting his mother, and when Wahb grew up he killed Pickett's cattle in delayed revenge.

It rained most of the night at Tower Falls—snowing higher up on the mountains to be crossed—but on the whole, we had a quiet night and sound sleep. When the rain ceased, about 9 o'clock A.M., September 16, we packed up and began the ascent of the Mt. Washburn range. For a few miles the trail followed an open ridge, exposing us to a northeast blizzard, accompanied by snow. After descending into the gulch, up which the trail leads to the pass in the range, the snow became deeper, and toward the summit of the range it was eighteen or twenty inches, knee-deep, which compelled us to dismount and lead the horses, as the ascent was very hard on them. In view of future possibilities, we made every effort to save their strength. It was one of the most laborious day's work of my experience.

When near the summit, going through open pine timber, we discovered a large bear approaching us. He was moving along the side of the steep mountain to the left, about on a level, and would have passed out of safe range. I immediately dismounted and cut across as rapidly as the snow and the ascent admitted, to intercept him. He had not discovered us. When within about one hundred yards, watching my opportunity through the timber, I fired at his side. He was hit, but not mortally. As my later experience told me, those bears when hit always either roll down hill or go "on the jump." On the jump this bear came, passing about twenty yards in our front. A cartridge was ready, and against Jack's injunction "Don't shoot," I fired; yet it failed to stop him, and Jack turned loose with his repeater, I shooting rapidly with my rifle. By the time the bear had reached the gulch he stopped, to go no further.

The excitement caused by this incident and my enthusiasm on killing my first grizzly—for I claimed the bear—dispelled at once all feelings of hardship and fatigue. The bear was a grizzly of about four hundred pounds weight, fat and with a fine pelt. We had not time to skin him, nor could the hide have been packed. After getting a few steaks, a piece of skin from over the shoulder and one of his fore-paws, we continued our laborious ascent of the mountain. Still excited by this incident, the work was now in the nature of a labor of love.

Passing over the summit and down a quarter of a mile, through snow still a foot deep, there were evident fresh pony tracks in the snow on the trail, made by an animal that had passed on up the gulch to our right. Jack was called up, and as we were seriously discussing the situation, a most unearthly sound proceeded from up the gulch, which caused us to grasp our rifles and feel for cartridge belts. In a short time that unearthly blast sounded forth again, from the same direction, but this time ending with a "he-haw, he-haw." The mystery was dispelled; the voice was recognized. It was the voice of the army mule. He had discovered by scent the presence of our outfit, and soon came trotting down the trail, the embodiment of joy and good fellowship. He turned out to be a big Missouri or Kentucky mule, sixteen hands high, that had broken down under his pack and had been turned loose by Howard's command and was endeavoring to follow on. He was a very forlorn looking animal. Our council of war decided he would soon perish in these deep snows. Jack Bean said the A. Q. M. at Fort Ellis was paying $30 for delivery of all such animals. I told him that I would help to carry him along and he could get the $30 for him; so we took him along and camped as soon as the snow became so little deep that the horses could feed in a small meadow, where camp was located.

There was an abundance of dry pine, and a rousing fire to dry us out was soon in full blast. The day had not been cold, but the rain, snow and wind made it appear so. We made fine beds of pine boughs, but I ate too much bear and did not rest well. That bear was taking post-mortem revenge on each of us.

1879

A Charging Grizzly
Philetus Norris

Here we get the full story of the big bear that Norris mentioned briefly in Part One. Here we also see the extent to which the park was viewed as a hunting reserve by some of its early administrators.

Interestingly, it would be hunters who would soon lead the campaign to have hunting eliminated in the park. Sportsmen, a leading force in the early conservation movement, were appalled by the hasty destruction of park animals, killed mostly by market hunters but also by regular visitors. By the late 1880s, Yellowstone Park was recognized as a reservoir of wildlife, the migrations of which to the surrounding country might serve as means to keep neighboring lands perpetually stocked with game. Though in practice the management of the animals and the hunters has never been simple, in principle the idea of the park as a game reservoir has held up quite well.

But that was long after Norris had his day near Obsidian Cliff with the big bear and wrote about it with such bravado.

In exploring routes, and hunting, killing, and packing game into camp, often through dense thickets of fallen timber, fire-hole basins, or yawning cañons, the hardships, dangers, and exposure to broiling sun and biting frost, or lonely camp-fire in unknown snowy regions, were ever chosen as pastime by our mountaineers, and the attendant incidents of such trips, including the nimble dodge from a wounded buck, or hasty tree-climbing from a ferocious grizzly, forms the standing basis for camp-fire stories or legends of the days agone. Such romance and enjoyment this season was, for the first time in the park, unalloyed by Indian raids or serious accidents or mishaps; but, as of little general interest, seldom mentioned in my reports or letters. But, of the animals killed during the past season, were some very large and fine elk, deer, sheep, and antelope, and a mountain lion, shot in the night to prevent his molesting our animals, which measured nearly 9 feet in length from lip whiskers to tip of tail, and the last of the six grizzlies killed by myself during the past season, was a remarkably large and fine one. A fine young horse, somewhat lamed by scalding in the fire holes, having been left near Obsidian Cañon, was killed by a grizzly, that, in devouring the carcass and fragments of game killed in the vicinity, continued to haunt the place. In trailing him in snow nearly knee deep some weeks afterwards, I killed two large antlered elks, but a few yards apart, and, it being nearly night, I only removed their entrails and camped alone near them, confident that bruin would visit them before morning. I then found that he had dragged the elk so near together as to leave only a space for a lair of boughs and grass between them, which he was intently finishing, when I, at a distance of 100 yards, opened fire with a Winchester rifle with fourteen ordinary bullets in the chamber and a dynamite shell—being all which I dared to use at once in the barrel. This I first gave him high in the shoulder, the shell there exploding and severing the main artery beneath the backbone. He fell, but instantly arose with a fearful snort or howl of pain and rage, but got four additional ordinary .44 claiber bullets in the shoulder, and nearly as many falls before discovering me, and then charged. Hastily inserting another dynamite shell, I, at a distance of about 50 yards, as he came in, sent it through his throat into his chest, where it exploded and nearly obliterated his lungs, again felling him; and as he arose, broke his neck with the seventh shot. Either one of these would have stiffened any other animal, and surely have soon proved fatal to him; but deeming delays just then dangerous, I peppered him lively. Finding Stephens across Beaver Lake, we returned with our saddle and pack animals, and after killing a pair of wood martens that were preying upon the carcasses, we dressed the animals, packing all pos-

Near Roosevelt Lodge, 1923.

sible of them 20 miles to our block-house at the Mammoth Hot Springs. We there found the hide of the bear just as spread out, without stretching, to be 8¾ feet long from tip of snout to roots of tail, and 6 feet 7 inches at its widest place; and from his blubber brought in, Stephens tried out 35 gallons of grease or oil. Its extraordinary size is the only reason for at all mentioning the animal in this report.

1902

Tourist Attacked by a Bear

The following account is in four brief parts. The first three appeared in a local newspaper, the Gardiner, Montana, *Wonderland,* on September 11 and 18 and October 30 (this one reprinted from another Montana paper), 1902. The last was written by Captain John Pitcher, the acting superintendent of the park, in his 1902 annual report.

Notice how the story evolves, first from a possible fatality, to a serious injury, and finally to a case of misconduct on the part of the victim. Notice also that we never do find out what species of bear it was. Judging from the accounts, it could have been either a grizzly or a black bear.

Pitcher's observation that the bears were becoming more numerous is probably an error. Eventually, the dumps probably attracted some bears from outside the park, but what he thought was an increase in bears was largely an increase in bears making themselves visible by eating at the dumps. The bears were always there; they just had little reason to show themselves. Yellowstone's total visitation was 13,433 in 1902, when this attack occurred (today it is typically more than two and a half million). Ten years later it was still only 22,970, but after World War I and the entry of the automobile into the park (starting in 1915), the numbers increased dramatically, providing more garbage for more bears.

September 11

R. E. Southwick, a tourist making the rounds of the park, was dangerously and perhaps fatally injured Saturday evening by being attacked by a bear. The party with whom Southwick was traveling had stopped for the night at the Lake hotel and during the early part of the evening he and his wife walked down the road for an evening stroll.

Not far from the hotel they met a cub bear and Southwick began petting it when he was attacked by the mother. He was thrown to the ground and the bear began tearing him to pieces.

Had it not been for the prompt action of his wife he would have been killed. She seized a club and wielded it upon the bear with such force that the animal was driven off. Parties from the hotel came to the rescue and carried the injured man to his room where it was found that he had received very severe, if not fatal injuries. He was bitten several times and the flesh was torn from his breast. One rib was broken and it is feared that his right lung is seriously injured. Southwick is a prominent business resident of Hart, Michigan.

September 18

The reported death of R. E. Southwick in the Park, who was injured by a bear, was evidently an error, and we are informed that he was able to leave the Park this week for his home.

October 30

"While it was a terrible and regrettable affair the injury of Mr. Southwick of Michigan from being torn by a bear in the Yellowstone park ought to teach people a lesson," said State Game Warden Scott.

"To tell the truth I am not particularly surprised over the affair. Many Park visitors seem to have no realization of the danger they run in monkeying with the animals. During the recent meetings of the state game wardens in the Park, I called the attention of Warden Fullerton of Minnesota one day to the freedom which a certain group of tourists was displaying towards the animals.

"I had a little experience one day that settled me. It was at the Geyser basin that I decided to leave bruin religiously alone. An unusually large animal was lumbering along and as he came in my direction I stopped to see what he would do. He kept coming and when he got within a few feet of me his hair began to bristle upon his back, an indication that he was mad. When I saw that hair stand up I dropped back and gave the right of way. If I had stood my ground I might not have been here today to tell of it."—Helena *Evening Herald*.

Black bear entertaining tourists, 1925. National Park Service photo.

The Bear-Feeding Regulation

The bear have certainly increased in numbers and continue to be a great source of interest for the tourists, for they can be seen at any time during the season, feeding at the garbage piles at the various hotels and permanent camps.

They are perfectly harmless as long as they are let alone and kept in a perfectly wild state, but when they are fed and petted, as some of them have been in the past, they lose all fear of human beings and are liable to do considerable damage to property and provisions at the various hotel and camp kitchens. They are also liable to frighten tourists by following them with the expectation of being fed. The black and brown bear are the ones that become the most friendly, and consequently give the most trouble. Three of these animals became such a nuisance during the past summer that it became necessary to have them killed.

It is a difficult matter to make some of the tourists realize that the bear in the park are wild, and that it is a dangerous matter to trifle with them. The possibility of an accident or injury to some indiscreet individual was anticipated, and on August 8, 1902, a circular was issued and posted at all of the hotels and permanent camps, absolutely prohibiting the interference with or molestation of bear or any other wild game in the park, etc. It was also forbidden for anyone to feed them except at the regular garbage piles. A violation of the instructions contained in this circular resulted in the serious injury of Mr. R. E. Southwick, a tourist from Hart, Michigan. Since the accident to Mr. Southwick, barriers have been put up at all of the garbage piles, and signs indicating the danger of approaching too near the bear have been posted.

1916

The Late Grizzly Bear Attacks in Yellowstone

J. A. McGuire

As this report shows, Yellowstone's grizzly bears were not seen as especially dangerous in 1916. The fatal attack on Frank (informally named "Jack" in the article) Welch, a teamster with the Army Quartermaster Corps, shocked some people into a more realistic view of the grizzly bear.

J. A. McGuire, then editor of *Outdoor Life* and a long-time crusader for bear conservation, revealed the rather simplistic view of the grizzly bear that prevailed in many enlightened circles at the time.

This attack occurred in the closing years of the U.S. Army's thirty-two-year administration of Yellowstone, and so McGuire's official source is the engineer then managing the road work in the park.

The unpredictability that McGuire found so disconcerting in 1916 is still a major part of Yellowstone bears. Keep in mind as you read these accounts by past "experts" that they have often been shown wrong in their beliefs and that we still have a lot to learn about the bears of Yellowstone.

The attacks upon human beings that have been committed by the big grizzly bear in Yellowstone National Park during the past summer and fall have aroused the fear of travelers and the interest of naturalists thruout the length and breadth of our country. Never before, in our

These very humanized Yellowstone bears appeared in F. Dumont Smith's book Summit of the World *(1909), which contained an account of the bears of the park. By this time, hunting was illegal and the bears were already celebrities, which only increased the risk of harmful encounters.*

present generation, has even the oldest mountaineer or woodsman in the United States known of a bear of any kind attacking men while they slept. In Alaska the big brown bears have been accused of doing so many unaccountable and extraordinary things that we would not care to stand sponsor for their good or their bad behavior, for we have never hunted them. But we know whereof we speak when we make the statement above recited regarding our bears in the States. Under ordinary circumstances a hunter is as safe to sleep out on a grizzly trail (where the fresh tracks of these animals are seen, made within only a few hours) as he would be in jail. Bears used to attack much more readily 100 years ago than they do now, or since they have learned from sad experience that the man smell is a very bad smell to run up against.

In the past few months there have been at least three distinct attacks made upon men in the Yellowstone Park by a grizzly bear. During the past summer Chub June was chewed up and badly lacerated by a grizzly near Sylvan Lake; Ned Frost and Ed Jones were terribly cut up by a grizzly near the Lake Hotel on August 14, while on September 7, Jack Welch, a freighter, was so badly torn up by a big grizzly at Ten-mile Spring, near Turbid Lake, that he died a few days later. Welch was the only one of the four men named whose injuries proved fatal.

There is no doubt in our mind or in the minds of those familiar with these attacks that they were all committed by the same bear. It might possibly have been a female and it is possible that in the earlier part of the year she was called upon to defend her young against a human, in which case she may have killed the man. If his acquaintance in the park were slight, or his identity obscure, he might not have been missed. Once having obtained the taste of human blood, she, or he, kept on attacking men whenever a favorable opportunity was afforded. If a female, her cub, or cubs (if any she had) were not with her when these attacks were made.

Many versions of the Welch attack have come to us thru newspapers and otherwise, but the most authentic and complete that we have received is from Maj. Amos A. Fries, in charge of engineering work in the park. According to Major Fries, Welch, who was driving a freight team, was camped at Ten-mile Spring, about sixty miles from headquarters. He and one of his helpers slept under the wagon and another helper slept on top. The wagon was loaded with hay and oats. "About 1 o'clock in the morning," writes Major Fries, "Mr. Devlin, who was alseep under the wagon with Mr. Welch, was awakened and heard a bear approaching. The bear started at Mr. Devlin, who threw his bedding and blankets at it, and yelled to wake up Mr. Welch. Mr. Devlin then clambered to the top of the load as fast as he could, while the bear ran to the opposite side of the wagon and grabbed Mr. Welch, who was a little slow in getting out from under the wagon. The bear pulled him out, but the two men on top of the load of forage threw a lunch box at the bear and began throwing the hay on him, which forced him to let Mr. Welch go.

"Mr. Welch then started to climb on the wagon, when the bear rushed and grabbed him and pulled him down. Again the bear was frightened off, but grabbed Mr. Welch a third time as he was trying to get on the wagon.

"It was probably during this last attack that he mangled Mr. Welch so terribly about the left shoulder, and on his side and abdomen. For the third time the two men on the wagon began tumbling bales of hay on the bear and drove him back, and then succeeded in getting Mr. Welch on top of the wagon.

"A few moments later, when one of the men was getting ready to go on horseback to Foreman Muse's camp at Sylvan Pass, eight miles beyond where Mr. Welch was attacked, an automobile came along with two men, and Mr. Welch and the two men with him were taken to Muse's camp. The men in the auto were requested to take Welch back to the lake, where there is a hospital, but they refused to do so, tho if they had Mr. Welch would have had a vastly better chance for life. Unfortunately, I have so far been unable to learn the names of the human brutes in the car."

An ambulance was sent from headquarters by direction of Major Fries and made the trip of sixty-four miles to the camp in a little less than four hours. Everything possible was done for him at the hospital, but to no avail. His body was buried at the post cemetery.

"The scene of this tragedy," said Major Fries, "was about six miles from where Ned Frost of the firm of Frost & Richard, who conduct camping parties thru the park, was attacked by a bear one night and badly torn. At the same time one of Mr. Frost's men was attacked and torn. However, the bear was scared away and both recovered. Frost & Richard were camped at Indian Pond, four miles from the Lake Junction, and about a quarter of a mile off the main Cody road.

"All agree that it was a grizzly in both cases, and it seems fair to assume that since the attacks took place in the same general locality, probably it was the same bear.

"Colonel Brett has given orders to hunt this bear and kill him. A few days later than this, a big grizzly bear came round Muse's camp, in Sylvan Pass, and under my instruction, a bait was set for him and fifteen sticks of 40 per cent dynamite were set off under his neck. Needless to say, the bear died at once."

1916

An Encounter with a Big Grizzly
Ned Frost

Two years after the Welch attack, Ned Frost, mentioned briefly in the previous story, told his own version of the events leading up to it. Frost was a prominent and respected guide and outdoorsman, and it is unfortunate that he did not write more about his adventures in the west.

Notice the extent to which bears were a part of everyday life in the park for Frost. Like many others, he considered dealing with their presence, and their attempts to get food, to be a part of the job.

Frost's account, which appeared in *Outdoor Life* in 1918, was followed by a brief editorial note, presumably by J. A. McGuire, still editor of the magazine. Notice McGuire's confident prediction that such an attack would not happen for another century. Wrong again, J. A. As of late 1990, four more people have been killed by bears in the park, as well as at least two more very near the park boundaries, and a number of other fatal attacks have occurred in other North American parks, by both black and grizzly bears.

In August, 1916, I had a most vivid illustration of what a real grizzly is capable of doing when he gets to pitting his strength against mere man. We had been out on a fishing and sightseeing trip in the Jackson Hole region and Upper Yellowstone country, coming into the Yellowstone National Park by way of the trail along the east side of the lake. On August 14th we arrived at Indian Pond. Our camp was about half a mile south of the Cody road to the park, and about four miles east of the Lake Hotel. This is a favorite camping ground. There were several automobiles camped at a cold spring near the road and around a point of timber out of sight of our camp. From our camp, however, to that of the autoists there was open meadow land. As it later developed, this was a very lucky thing for two of us that night.

For over fifteen years I have been conducting camping parties thru the Yellowstone, and during this time I had become, as I supposed, thoroly familiar with the habits of the park bear. I knew about what to expect from him and about how far to go in driving him away from the bacon, ham, sugar and other provisions. Many are the hams and slabs of bacon I have donated to the ursus family of night prowlers during these years. Many a time have I run them off with clubs or firebrands; while on the contrary, many a time has some old silver-tip bluffed me out by showing that he was there for results and there was nothing for me to do but to stand by and let him help himself. But this I had never held against them, for I always figured that as an attraction to the tourist they offset all the damage they did to my camps. However, I always took the precaution of sleeping right with the grub pile, figuring that I myself was safe from attack if I did not put up too stiff a defense in case of an assault by a grizzly.

On this particular night, August 14, 1916, we had noticed some unusually large grizzly tracks around camp. Consequently we had sat up rather later than usual around the camp fire, reassuring Mr. and Mrs. Frothingham of Boston, whom I was guiding on this trip, that there was absolutely no danger; that bears were perfectly harmless if you did not molest them at their prowling or predatory excursions; and that there was not a case on record where a bear had made an unprovoked attack on a human being. So, putting up the Frothinghams' bed tent some distance from the main camp, Shorty, the horse wrangler, Jonesy, the cook, and I made our beds down in the open, one on each side of the pack containing the provisions.

It was a clear moonlight night, but rather cool and cheerless, so I put an extra heavy canvas pack cover over my sleeping bag just before

I turned in. This I have often thought since may have been the means of saving my life. Shorty, Jonesy and I had been working together for years thru the Yellowstone and the hunting country. We felt no uneasiness whatever as we lay down to rest, and were all sound asleep almost immediately.

At about half an hour after midnight we were aroused by the most bloodcurdling yells I ever heard come from human kind. Raising myself in my sleeping bag, I saw there in the bright moonlight about fifteen feet away from me a huge grizzly. He had Jonesy by the back and was shaking him, bed and all, as a terrier shakes a rat. Yelling at the top of my voice, as Shorty was also doing, I threw my pillow. As the white mass landed just in front of him, the bear flung Jonesy to the ground and started back. His fiery little green balls of eyes caught sight of me as I sat up in bed waving my arms over my head in a vain attempt to scare him. Then he made a lunge for me. This was one of the times when the human mind works quickly. Throwing myself back and jerking the bedding over me, I drew my knees up and held the covers over my head and throat. With my other hand folded across my breast, I waited for what seemed an age as the beast made the two or three jumps necessary to reach me. I felt his fangs rasping on the bones about my knees almost with the first impact. Here was where I believe I experienced more or less of the same feelings of the soldiers going "over the top" for the first-line German trenches. Time after time he hurled me thru the air, always getting farther from the camp into the dark shadows of the thick timber, while the voices of the yelling Shorty and Jonesy grew fainter and fainter.

The covers were finally pulled from my head and the gleaming fangs and drooling jaws were within a foot and a half of my eyes. The hot breath of the old devil had a very repugnant odor, which seemed almost to choke me, and I wondered just how it was going to feel when he would finally loose his hold on my legs and sink his great teeth into my exposed throat. I remember thinking it wouldn't be a very hard death, for if he would just get me by the neck everything would be over quickly.

That I am alive today I attribute to a lucky fluke. After shaking and carrying me along several times he finally got a mouthful of sleeping bag only and with a vicious shake threw me clear of the bag, like a potato out of a hole in the sack. Head over heels I went for several yards, landing under some low-hanging jack pine branches. I grasped these, intending to climb the tree, but my lacerated knees refused to bear my weight, so I went hand over hand—to the very top, you may be sure, and the wonder is I am not going yet.

The bear was still busy looking for me in the bed. By this time Shorty had made a dash for his night horse which was staked near by; Jonesy, still yelling, upset stove and table, with all the dishes in camp, and with all the racket and disturbance, the old boy finally shambled off into the timber. The minute he was gone Shorty beat it to the automobile camp and within twenty minutes we were on the way to the Lake Hotel. In less than an hour two doctors and a nurse were working on us. Jonesy had four places in his back stitched up; and his face was sort of smeared sidewise a bit where old Bruin had stepped on it. I had six wounds in my legs sewed up. In one the main artery, the size of a lead pencil, was exposed for two inches, but not ruptured. If it had been, I should have bled to death in ten minutes.

Did that old boy intend to get me? Two weeks later he proved it by attacking two other campers. One of them was badly wounded, but was rescued by his comrades. They were trying to lift the victim to the top of a load of baled hay when the bear charged again and took his man, completely disemboweling him, and poor Jack Welch died the next day.

As a souvenir of my experience I suffer from cold knees when the thermometer goes down very far, as the circulation seems to have been badly interfered with around my kneecaps. This is the only lingering reminder of my adventure, except a desire to wage war to the death on any member of the family of ursus horribilis, from cubhood to old age.

And only a few weeks ago I had the pleasure of exploding a .280 Ross in an extra big old boy, one dark stormy night (and not in the Yellowstone Park either) who was nosing around my bed within twenty feet. I don't sleep well any more with those old devils spooking around my bunk, and I can fairly smell one if he comes within miles.

Note.—There is no more truthful or reliable man, upon whose shoulders should fall the task of relating such an encounter as described, than Ned Frost. His life for thirty-five years (and every year of it) has been spent hunting, trapping, camping and traveling in Wyoming's big game fields, and during that time—like all men who have lived continuously in the haunts of the game, he had learned that the wild animals were harmless if you left them alone and used good judgment in dealing with them. But here was a most extraordinary and exceptional case. Never before in the history of the bears of our country had we ever heard of such a one as this. Nor had Mr. Frost or any of the old timers heard of such a surprising action by a bear. The general consensus of opinion among Wyoming guides and hunters and which is also shared by Mr. Frost—is that this bear some time, just previous to the attack described, killed a human—whether in defense of young, or self defense, or what of course is not known or to be even guessed at—and, having learned that it could kill and successfully "get away with it," the animal lost fear of man entirely. It is possible that some lone traveler or else some one unknown in that region might have been killed whose presence was not missed. At any rate, the two or three unprovoked attacks that occurred in Yellowstone Park that year (1916) were all made by this bear—that fact has been established. We predict it will be 100 years before another such incident will happen at the hands of bears anywhere in the United States—and, if the Fates decree that we shall be free of such a danger for that length of time, of course they shall never occur, as 100 years hence the few wild animals we now have are apt to be in steel cages or too tame to attempt violence. —Editor.

1920

Bear Boldness
Milton Skinner

Milton Skinner, a National Park Service naturalist in the 1920s, spent many years in and around Yellowstone and eventually wrote several books about the park and its wildlife. His little volume *Bears in the Yellowstone,* which appeared in 1925, is still entertaining reading. For its time, it was a reasonably good effort and showed great sympathy and affection for the bears.

Here he tells two stories, one from 1920 and one from 1915, of bears trying to get into park buildings. This sort of raid was common for many years in the park, and quite often the bears were successful, though usually there was not quite as much drama associated with their assaults as young George experienced in the following tale.

In the fall of the year, just before the bears enter their long winter sleep, they are intensely hungry and will go to extremes to get food. In October of 1920 I was at the Basin Ranger Station. While peacefully sleeping during the night of the twenty-second, I suddenly awakened to find myself sitting bolt upright on my cot listening to faint crack-lings and bumps that seemed to come from the rear. Stopping only to catch up a handy axe I rushed out to see what was the matter. I did not see the bear but his tracks in the snow showed who the marauder was. It was too dark and cold to see just what damage he had done, but in the morning I had a better chance. From his tracks I found this bear had come up behind the Station and circled it three or four times, each time stopping to try the kitchen door. But that door was barred and resisted his efforts. Then he had turned his attention to the woodshed. This was merely a shell of a building with its siding nailed to the outside of the studding. As is usually the case, each board of this siding overlapped the next lower board and so afforded a hold for the bear's claws. By hooking his claws under the edge of the lower board and heaving upward he had torn off three boards and opened up the whole inside of the shed. Apparently he had entered the shed and was preparing to break open an old refrigerator box when my sudden jump from bed scared him away. So he got nothing. But he came back again on the night of the twenty-fourth and again on the twenty-seventh. Each time the noise I made scared him off so promptly that I neither saw him nor surprised him at his work. Yet he was so strong and dexterous that each time he got from three to five of those boards off before I could get out although I had nailed them fast as securely as I could each time.

But a far more striking example of bear boldness—this time grizzlies—so surprisingly daring and contrary to the animals' usual caution that, for many years, I never ventured to tell it, occurred here in the Yellowstone. In May of 1915 I visited a faraway cabin where a young chap was spending a lonely time caring for horses at a stage relay station. He told me he had been visited a few nights previously by four grizzlies bent on breaking into his meathouse, and showed me the battle ground inside, and the holes in the sod roof. It was in the spring and the bears, only just recently from their winter's sleep, were ravenously hungry. During the early evening, they were heard shuffling about the station, but as they made no overt attack and bears were a common occurrence, they were not molested. They became so quiet that my friend concluded they had gone away and went to bed at his usual hour. Some time during the dead of night he heard a thump-thump on the roof and soon located it over the meatshed that adjoined his bunkroom. He had a rifle, but had used up all his cartridges during the winter on coyotes and had neglected to get any more. But as the sound increased in volume he caught up his lantern and a handy pitchfork and dashed into the meatroom. This was a stout log lean-to with no other opening than the door into the bunkroom. It needed only an instant to show that the bears were on the roof and *digging through!* The roof was of clay and sod and was still frozen, for there had been no fire under it, although the sun had melted the winter snow from the top. Still more fortunately the split poles supporting the earth were heavy and stronger than usual and overlaid with thin sheet iron, so that the bears had much more trouble than they would have had ordinarily. It was a difficult job but in time they got through the clay, bent back the sheet iron and began to spring the poles apart. Then began a long, hard fight. Whenever a crack showed, the pitchfork was jabbed up through, and whenever it struck a paw or the bears' underparts it brought snarls and "woofs." The paws were so tough, very little damage was done to them, but once in a while a fortunate jab brought blood from nose, breast, or belly. Occasionally a nose or a paw came down through a crack, but a steady clubbing on them caused their withdrawal and more howls. The bears would not give up the contest, but now that the strong odor of the ham, bacon and fresh meat came direct to their nostrils they redoubled their efforts. The poles were strong and the sheet iron protected the roof, but still it is likely that they would have succeeded if they could have held out long enough, for George's violent efforts to keep all four bears busy in different parts of the roof were fast tiring him. There were many times during the long night when it seemed as if he must give up, but finally dawn began to break. At first the bears hardly noticed it, but after a time they became less active and shortly after sunrise they jumped down and retired, growling, to the woods. But the roof was a wreck. The frozen clay was scattered in chunks all about the building, the sheet iron bent, twisted and torn by tooth and claw into a tangle of metal shreds, and the stout roof poles were twisted, clawed and sprung apart until I wondered the bears had not tumbled through. George had not fully recovered when I saw him and he told me he was so exhausted that he doubted if he could have held out for another hour.

Part Three

TOURISTS, SOLDIERS, AND RANGERS

In *The Bears of Yellowstone,* I describe the relationship between park visitors and bears as "an American romance." It has been a wild and stormy affair, too, with much more comic relief than most romances.

In 1886, the U.S. Cavalry was assigned to protect the park, and the soldiers almost immediately found themselves caught between the visitors and the bears. Later, following the creation of the National Park Service in 1916, rangers found themselves in the same awkward position.

During the half-century or so represented by the following accounts, bear watching became institutionalized to an almost unbelievable extent. From the first visitors who found their way to unsupervised garbage dumps in the 1890s, it was a fast trip to the thousands who attended evening festivities at the formalized feeding grounds, complete with grandstands and ranger commentary, of the 1920s and 1930s. In the course of the trip, the bears of Yellowstone were turned into performers on a stage that had very little to do with their wild home, but that had a great deal to do with public tastes in entertainment.

Fortunately, public tastes do change. Growing disapproval among park enthusiasts and scientists led to the closure of the public feeding grounds in the 1940s. After that, bears still ate garbage, but did so out of sight of the visitors. Closing these hidden dumps did not occur for another thirty years and was accompanied by great controversy, but that's a story for other books.

1891

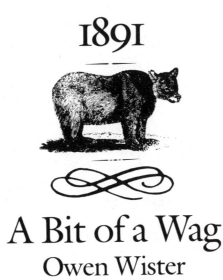

A Bit of a Wag
Owen Wister

Owen Wister, author of *The Virginian* (1902) and other western novels, visited Yellowstone several times in the 1880s and 1890s and wrote about it with the same lively wit that made him such a popular commentator on the west. These episodes suggest that it was only a short time after hunting was prohibited that the bears learned the convenience of the garbage dumps and that it was even a shorter time after that that park visitors discovered the peculiar joys of watching bears eat trash.

Wister's "cinnamon" bear was, of course, the brown color phase of the black bear. Many early observers referred to the brown ones as cinnamon, and some seem even to have considered them a separate species.

Long before 1896 the hotels were larger, and the education of the bears had begun. They were now aware that man did not shoot them and they had discovered that campers carried good things to eat. One night in 1891 our sleep was murdered by sudden loud rattling and clashing of our tin plates and other hardware. We rushed out of the tent into silence and darkness. In the morning our sugar sack lay wounded, but still with us. Macbeth while dragging at it had tumbled the hardware about him. He was not educated enough to stand that and had taken to the woods. Another bear took to a tree that week.

As dusk was descending, campers found him in suspicious proximity to their provender and raised a shout. The shouting brought us and others not to the rescue, but to the highly entertaining spectacle of a tree surrounded by fascinated people waving their arms, and a bear sitting philosophically above their din. Night came on, the campers went to bed, and the bear went away. Many years have now gone since the bears discovered the treasures that are concealed in the garbage piles behind the hotels. I walked out once in the early evening at the Lake Hotel and counted twenty-one bears feasting. I saw a bear march up to a tourist and accept candy from his hand, while his wife stood at a safe distance, protesting vainly, but I think rightly. I saw the twenty-one bears suddenly cease feasting and withdraw to a short distance. Out of the trees came a true grizzly, long-snouted and ugly; and while he selected his dinner with ostentatious care and began to enjoy it, a cinnamon bear stole discreetly, as if on tip-toe, toward the meal he had left behind him. He got pretty near it, when the grizzly paused in eating and merely swung his head at him — no more than that; in a flash the cinnamon had galloped humpty-dumptily off and sat down watching. He came back presently; and the scene was re-enacted three times before I had enough of it and left; each time when the cinnamon bear had reached a certain point the grizzly swung his head, and this invariably sufficed. It is my notion that the cinnamon was a bit of a wag.

1894

Bears in the
Yellowstone Park
from *Forest and Stream*

The casual and regular dealings between bears and visitors in early Yellowstone seem unreal to modern visitors, who are constantly reminded to be careful with their ice chests, to keep clean camps, and to otherwise do everything possible to avoid bears. But in Yellowstone's early days, bears were a fact of life, and almost anyone seemed free to do a little "bear management," as the coach driver did in the following account.

Not long after this episode, the officers in charge of the park took steps to prevent cruelty to the bears. Occasional abuses of bears continued for many years.

We extract the following from a private letter written by a gentleman recently returned from the Park:

When we reached the Lake Hotel the clerk at the desk asked us if we wished to see a bear, as he could show us one after we had finished dinner. We went with him to a spot some two hundred feet back of the hotel, where was deposited the swill and refuse. It was then a little after sunset. We waited some moments, when the clerk, taking his watch out of his pocket, said, "It is strange he has not

75

come down; he is now a little over due." Before he had replaced his watch, he exclaimed, "Here he comes now," and we saw descending slowly from a hill close by a very large black bear. The bear continued to approach us, when I said to the clerk, "Had we better not get behind the timber; he will be frightened off should he see us?" He answered, "No, he will not be frightened in the least," and continued to converse with us in a loud voice. We were then standing in the open close by the swill heap, and the bear continued coming toward us, there being no timber intervening. We did not move, but continued talking. The bear came up to us without hesitation, diverging slightly from his direct route to the swill heap so as to approach nearer to us. He surveyed us leisurely with his nose in the air, got our scent, and seeming content that we were only harmless human beings, turned slowly away and went to the swill heap, where he proceeded to make a meal. We watched him for quite a while, when a large wagon passing along the road nigh to where we stood, the bear stopped feeding and went toward the hotel, in the direction in which the wagon was traveling. Our guide exclaimed, "He has gone to visit the pig sty," and in a little while we were satisfied this was so by hearing a loud outcry of, "bar, bar," which we afterward found proceeded from a Chinaman, one of whose special duties it was to keep the bears out of the pig sty.

After the departure of the black bear, we retraced our steps, but before getting to the hotel I suggested to my friend Dell that if we returned to the refuse pile we might see another bear. We accordingly went back on the trail to within a few yards of where we stood before. When we stopped we heard, in the timber nearby, a great noise as if dead pine branches were being smashed, and there emerged into the open a large grizzly. Although he was not quite so familiar as the black bear, he showed no hesitation but walked straight toward us and the object of his visit—the swill. Before reaching his destination, however, he stopped and squatted down on his haunches, calmly surveying the scene before him. The reason why he stopped became at once apparent. From the same hill down which the black bear had come we saw another grizzly, larger than the first, moving toward us at a rapid gait, in fact, on a lope, while the first grizzly regarded him with a look not altogether friendly or cordial. The second bear did not stop an instant until he reached the swill heap, where he proceeded to devour everything in sight without any regard to us or his fellow squatted nearby. The latter apparently had had some experience on a former occasion which he was not desirous of repeating.

Three men coming through the timber toward us, made a considerable racket, and the two bears moved off at no rapid gait in opposite directions. Until I left the spot I could see one of them on the edge of the timber, looking toward us, and no doubt, waiting for more quiet before partaking of the delights before him. When the three men joined us and were talking about the late departed, one of them shouted, "Here come two more," and before we could realize it we saw two good-sized cinnamons at the feast. They paid no attention whatever to us, but were entirely absorbed in finishing up what the other bears had left. By this time it was fast becoming dark and we returned to the hotel. I should have said that we measured the distance from the nearest point from the black bear to where we stood, and found it to be exactly twenty-one feet. The other bears were but a few yards further from us.

The squirrels, of which there were quite a number, were most diverting. Their presence alone added a playful element to a scene made solemn by twilight and the huge animals passing to and fro. We could tell when a bear was approaching by the chattering of bunny. He would run along the ground toward the bear with tail defiantly uplifted, jerking his head from side to side and scolding incessantly. I believe his anger was increased because the bear took no notice of him and yet he never allowed his animosity to lead him far from a place of security which he sought whenever his great enemy moved toward him. Doubtless his hatred was due to the remembrance of many hoards of piñon nuts, laboriously shelled and stored away for winter use and ruthlessly devoured by the huge and ugly beast.

When we entered the hotel we entertained our friends with an account of what we had seen, and had there not been three eyewitnesses, we probably would have been entirely disbelieved. As we were giving our account, a man came into the room and said, "If you want some fun come outside; we have got a bear up a tree." We went outside of the hotel and not over forty feet from it found a black bear in a pine tree. It seems, the wagon I have mentioned, had been stopped at the pine tree, and left there after the horses had been taken out. The owner, returning to his wagon found the bear in it, and this was the explanation why the bear had so suddenly taken to the tree.

The animal was considerably smaller than the one we had seen earlier; in fact it was not more than half as large, but still full grown. Quite a number of packers and teamsters stood about, amusing themselves by making the bear climb higher, till at last one of them asked our driver, Jim McMasters, why he did not climb the tree and shake the bear out. It was quite dark and McMasters replied that he would not mind doing so if there were enough daylight for him to see. His companions continuing to banter him, he finally said, "I believe I'll go up anyhow," and up he went, climbing, however—instead of the tree the bear had ascended—a companion tree which grew alongside of the other, the two not being more than a foot or so apart and the branches interlaced. We soon lost sight of McMasters and of the bear also, for as Jim climbed the bear would climb too, until at last they both reached the top of their respective perches; when we heard Jim cry out, "Boys, he's got to come down; I can reach him." With that he proceeded to break off a small branch of his tree and we could hear him whack the bear with it and also could hear the bear remonstrating with a very unpleasant voice, at times approaching a roar. But at last the bear seemed to have made up his mind that it was better to come down than stay up and be whacked with a pine branch, so down he came, but not with any great rapidity, stopping at every resting place until Jim came down too and gave him a little persuading.

We could now see the action, but its dangerous features were lost sight of in its amusing ones. Jim had climbed on the tree down which the bear was descending, and when he was not persuading the bear he was pleading with us, somewhat as follows: "Now, boys, don't throw up here, and don't none of you hit him until he gets down. If he should make up his mind to come up again he'd clean me out, sure." After each speech of this sort he would move down to where the bear was and apply his branch, whereupon both the man and the animal would come down a few pegs lower. At last the bear was almost at the ground. We all formed a circle around the tree prepared to give both man and beast a reception when they should alight. The beast came first, and every fellow who had anything in the way of wood in his hand gave the bear admonishing blows that he might not return to the wagon again. Jim, when he got down, did not seem to think that he had done anything more than if the bear had been a possum, which he had shaken out of the tree. And so ended our bear symposium of that evening, an experience one would fail to meet with even if he stopped at the best appointed hotel at Saratoga or other fashionable resort. Jim told me— and after what I had seen him do I did not doubt his word—that he had met this spring thirteen bears near the hotel at the cañon at one time.

1902

Bear Studies
in the Yellowstone
Addison Neil Clark

There was very little real study in the following account, but it does provide
a good account of life in park camps when bears were accustomed to getting
plenty of human food. We also see the military managers in action, removing
a bear that got into trouble too often to suit the author.

Even in these early days, a few people realized that the bears weren't
to blame; they were only taking advantage of an unusual food source, exactly
the behavior they had evolved to display so well. Unprotected food was
the problem, and it would not be solved for another 70 years.

To the Yellowstone Park, undoubtedly, belongs the distinction of
being the American paradise of the bear. Numbers of writers have
described various summer phases of bear life in this unique corner
of our country, so that readers are more or less familiar with Bruin
as the observing summer tourist may see him—contented in his undis-
turbed possession of sundry "happy hunting grounds" in the refuse
heaps adjoining hotels and tourist camps throughout the park. To
these, every summer evening brings a host of bears; black bears,
cinnamon bears and "silvertips;" bears great and bears small; the

sociable bear, and the grouchy fellow, who refuses to show himself if the group of sightseers grows too large or edges too close to his dinner-table.

The sociable class included "Dewey," with an amiable disposition and an excessive fondness for sweets. "Dewey" belonged to the cinnamon tribe. Other bears, mostly black ones, came to enjoy feasts in the same back yard, but they came cautiously and in dead of night. To the Cañon Hotel, however, a mile up the hill from this camp, came a delegation of fifteen or more bears every evening; and among these were some "silvertips" of no small stature.

The difference is great indeed, however, between a Yellowstone bear in the height of the tourist season, with a choice menu from which to select, and the same fellow a few weeks after all hotels and camps have closed and the demand for ursine delicacies is far in excess of supply.

During the summer and fall of 1902, I was employed by the government as an engineer in the work of extending the system of coach roads in the park. I was fortunate in being stationed in what is both the grandest part of the park scenically, and perhaps the best for the study of its wild animals—that is to say, the vicinity of the Grand Cañon and Mount Washburn, almost within sound of that king of western waterfalls, the Lower Yellowstone. Here one may, within a radius of ten miles from these falls, come into close contact with bear, deer, elk, antelope, mountain sheep and beaver, to say nothing of the ever cautious, yet inquisitive, coyote. But it is with the bear and his doings that this narrative is solely concerned.

We pitched our first camp early in July, some two miles from the Cañon Hotel and near the edge of a beautiful mountain "park" or meadow at the forks of Cascade Creek. The latter is a clear, cold stream, peaceful enough at that point, but three miles farther down hurling itself over Crystal Falls to run brawling into the Yellowstone at a point midway between the upper and lower falls. Our crew was a typical "construction gang" about eighty strong; it consisted of a small survey party in charge of myself, and the construction party proper in charge of a genial, rotund North Dakotan.

We rejoiced from the outset in an excellent cook—a grizzled old Westerner with fierce gray mustaches, and a murderous looking slouch hat, beneath which twinkled a pair of the most kindly of eyes. Him

Public attitudes about park bears were further complicated by the frequent presence of captive bears in the park. "Juno," raised from a cub in the late 1920s (and pictured here in about 1926 with Ranger Ed Bruce), was one of these domesticated bears that were more pets than wild animals.

we christened "Dad" at once, in tribute to his being the senior member of the party.

Dad lived in constant apprehension of the bears, and nightly barricaded the doors of the cook and commissary tents with dish-pans, oil-cans, pie-plates—anything that would make a racket if disturbed. How efficient was his alarm system we discovered while prowling for pie late one evening. We failed to reach the pie bin, but we knocked down several square yards of tinware and made several cubic yards of unearthly noise, which brought Dad promptly to the scene waving a huge cleaver. We made peace with him finally by praising his alarm system, which fortunately was never sprung by other than two-legged marauders.

As a matter of fact, we underrated the discrimination of the Yellowstone bears in looking for trouble so early in the season, with our camp but two miles from the Cañon Hotel; for the menu offered at our refuse pit was hardly up to the standard set in the rear yard of that hostelry. Only once at that camp did we hear from them.

About 9 o'clock one July evening we were lying around the camp-fire, telling and listening to bear stories. The tents of the foreman, sub-foreman, time-keeper, rodmen and myself formed an irregular circle upon a flat piece of ground that broke the hillside. Just at the edge of the meadow and not a hundred yards from our fire was the cook's refuse pit; and, as a vivid illustration to the story just being told, there came suddenly from that direction a most hair-raising roar, followed by a series of ugly growls and a second roar in a deeper key.

We leaped to our feet as one man and looked one another in the face, wonderingly. It was a brilliantly moonlit night, and as we ran to the edge of our little clearing and peered through the trees we saw a pair of dark forms lurching about the edge of the pit; and there came thence a medley of growls and snarls calculated to elevate the hair of the most phlegmatic. It was merely a difference of opinion, we learned later, between a black bear and a silvertip, as to which should precede the other at the feast—a discarded side of bacon, for which delicacy Bruin has a decided fondness.

This, the opening gun of the bear campaign, proved a blank shot, so to speak, for at that camp there were no more advances made upon us. Not even audible evidence did Bruin give thereafter of his existence, though often in the mornings the workmen would find in the soft surface of the newly graded roadbed the imprints of his great padded paws.

Shortly after this episode we moved our headquarters some two miles up the line. Our second camp was situated at a point where the old Washburn Trail crosses the east fork of Cascade Creek; here we lived in absolute peace as far as bears were concerned until we began to think of moving on to a third camp.

Dad grew careless during this reign of peace; and although the main supply of meat was always hoisted into a tree at nightfall, a small quarter left on terra firma one evening proved too much for Bruin's self restraint. He came, in might and great numbers, and not only succeeded in making short work of that but in ripping open a case of bacon as well; and what a fight he and his chums had over that bacon! Its noise and fervor, and the loss of our supplies, made us decide to post a night-watchman thereafter near the cook-tent. Furthermore, from that time on Dad kept the bacon in the tent which served as his boudoir; and it was well, for the stolen sweets of the night before had whetted Bruin's appetite for more. He told, I believe, every bear within a radius of ten miles all about that bacon. They all wanted some, and only the watchman's great fire beside the cook tent prevented their charging for it in a body. He waked a few of the "boys," and they amused themselves all night, and possibly amused the bears as well, by throwing brands of burning wood at the twin coals that glowed here and there in the darkness, below the refuse pit and across the tiny creek. Finding the watchman's squad too vigilant for them, and having a wholesome dread of fire, they sampled the contents of the refuse pit itself and rattled tin cans and snarled over sharp edges until dawn. A few days after this we packed our impedimenta and pushed on to our third and last camp of the season. It was pitched beside a beautiful but nameless stream which runs from the rocky sides of Dunraven Peak—a stream of remarkable clearness and sweetness, which supplied us with the best drinking water imaginable.

As before, after our moving day we rejoiced in a long period of absolute peace, by night as well as by day, but we had learned our lesson, and slept with one eye open. Dad's confidence in all that moved about by night had been sadly shattered, as I discovered while rummaging in his cake box one night for a midnight lunch. An unlucky move set a pile of tin cups to dancing about the table and brought the old man out of bed fully armed, with a whoop that aroused his nearer neighbors and caused me to execute a hasty retreat through the other end of the mess tent and a long detour up the hill to my own.

The day following this "ado about nothing" was the close of the tourist season. Knowing that the entire tribe of bears in the vicinity of the Grand Cañon would be on the lookout for other sources of supply as soon as that at the hotel had been exhausted, we began to lay plans for handling our side of the campaign.

Our refuse pile at this camp had been injudiciously placed too near the commissary tent, being but little more than a hundred feet down the stream. Had all of our visitors been like the first two that came, this would have made no difference and all would have been well. These were, respectively, a black she-bear and her cub—the latter a precocious youngster of but a season's growth, whom we forthwith dubbed "Sonny." They came often together, but sometimes singly; and Master Cub's solitary visits were always a source of much amusement to a number of the crew, who would close in on him and drive him up a tree—he always selected the same tree—where he would sit and cry, pitifully but comically, like a baby for his mamma. The "boys" persisted in this sport, in the face of warning from others, whose experience with bears had been more extensive, until one evening Sonny's cries produced results.

Up to this time his mother had always been most lady-like in her behavior, coming, eating and going without looking to the right or left; but who can blame her for finally losing her temper? At a particularly strident howl from the tormented "Sonny," there was a sudden crashing in the underbrush across the creek; then, from somewhere, came a mass of black fur in which blazed two red coals of eyes, swiftly as though fired from a cannon. Straight at the group of Sonny's tormentors she hurled her black bulk, with a snarl that scattered them as effectually as would a cyclone—and she looked and sounded not a little like one. Sonny forthwith clambered down from his perch and shambled up to his parent, telling her all about it while she both caressed and cuffed him; his erstwhile tormentors gazing in wonder and trepidation from a safe distance up the hill.

Later that evening—it had now been some ten days since the hotels had closed—our ears were saluted by sounds similar to those which had served to elaborate our first evening of bear stories. It sounded as though half a dozen bears were at it this time, and the empty cans rattled a vigorous accompaniment to a wild medley of snarls and growls.

The more curious among the crew crept down toward the commissary tent, and on their return reported the woods full of bears. Dad's apprehensions were at once wrought up to a most acute pitch. He insisted that there should be no sleep for him unless a guard were placed over the commissary at night; and as a cook must sleep or be ill tempered, and an ill-tempered cook means trouble in the mess tent, we catered to his feelings and incidentally to our own by placing between the refuse pile and the commissary tent the desired sentry—a huge, good-natured Montana "cow puncher" who rejoiced in the airy name of Spray coupled with six feet and three inches of height.

The commissary tent stood at the lower end of the cook and mess tents, which had been pitched end to end to form one continuous covering; and below stood Dad's tent, in which, by the way, he still kept the bacon.

Spray knew bears somewhat himself, and promptly kindled a huge fire—using as fuel some ample logs which the boys aided him in placing—directly in line with the bear rendezvous, and in such wise as to throw, when burning well, a strong light in that direction. These details attended to, the majority of the crew bethought themselves of the morrow's work and sought their respective tents; only a few remaining to "josh" Spray and peer curiously through the fire light in an attempt to catch a glimpse of the marauders.

By 11 o'clock only the watchman and his fire remained to protect our interests, and the morning dawned without further incident. So quiet had been his vigil that Spray argued that there was no necessity for further night watches; but Dad overheard his argument from afar and entered such a vigorous protest, coupled with a most winning invitation to Spray to draw upon any portion of his larder during the night, that the cowboy, partial to things edible, made preparation to put in another night on duty. And on this night there appeared on the scene a new character—an immense silvertip that proved the liveliest visitor of the season—and the "turn" that she did nearly left Spray gray-headed.

He had been fairly vigilant until long past midnight; and with the exception of a slight disturbance of the empty cans at the pit, nothing of interest had occurred. The fire had burned down to a bed of glowing coals and, becoming drowsy, Spray had fallen asleep between it and Dad's tent, leaning against the latter.

Somewhere in the wee sma' hours, those of us sleeping nearest to the cook tent were awakened by a blood-stirring yell that brought us from among warm blankets with visions of Spray's anatomy rent by bear's claws, and other horrible thoughts; for there had been but one yell followed by an interval of dead silence. A crash in the undergrowth beside by tent was followed by a glimpse of Spray careering through the moonlight-flecked clearing like one possessed, laying a course for the foreman's tent. Jumping into a pair of trousers, and an ulster, I hastened to the same point, to find the erstwhile guard the center of a small and excited group, his eyes bulging and his chest heaving like that of a race-horse as he panted out his story.

He had, he thought, been asleep but a few minutes when some-one attempted to turn him over. Paying no attention, he felt another and more persistent shove, whereupon he let drive a volley of Mon-tana invective, sitting upright and looking about for the meddler. What he saw brought forth the yell that had in turn brought us forth; for beside and almost over him stood a shaggy silvertip, dividing her attention between the odor of salt bacon from within the tent and what he afterwards discovered to be the cause of her attempted familiarity—nothing more nor less than his paper of sandwiches, upon which he had been inadvertently lying. She looked like a mountain in the moonlight and what firelight remained, and without waiting to think of Dad or the bacon our sentinel rent the air with his voice and proceeded to place a more comfortable distance between himself and his visitor. As for Dad, although the night was cold he had appeared among the group in the foreman's tent almost as soon as I had—clad in some amazing red flannels and nothing more.

This was too much, decided the council. Hunting bears is excel-lent sport; but being hunted by bears and at the same time prevented by the strict Park laws from retaliating was more than Western con-stitutions could stand. The next morning we sent word of our troubles to the officer in charge of the cavalry detachment stationed at the falls. He telephoned the situation to Fort Yellowstone, and Colonel Pitcher—superintendent of the Park and legal guardian of its wild animals—issued orders that, should Madame Silvertip continue her mischief-making, she would be shot; but not unless she gave further trouble. The soldiers were to be the executioners, incidentally, a pro-vision which caused much fuming and chafing among the Nimrods of the crew.

That night was selected as the one on which to "give her another chance;" and knowing that some excitement was afoot, quite a knot of spectators gathered about the watch-fire after supper. Their laughter and noise served to keep the bears aloof and in the background until,

Filming a black bear near Lake Yellowstone, about 1923.

at a late hour, the group separated to go to bed, chaffing Spray for having seen visions the night before and stirring up excitement over nothing. The giant held his peace and let them chaff, knowing well why they had not seen bears. Then he settled himself comfortably on the campward side of his fire to pass judgment as to whether the further conduct of his visitor of the night before should warrant her death.

I had been reading in my tent all the evening, and at about eleven o'clock decided that I was hungry. Slipping into the upper end of the mess tent I quickly found the pie case (a location familiar through much experience) and a moment later, with a piece of pie in each hand, walked around the commissary tent to share it with Spray. As I came into the light of the fire a clash among the cans saluted me, followed by a convincing, "Woof! woof!"

"Look out!" yelled Spray; and I did. Coming straight for me on the run, her back bristling and her ugly little eyes glaring, was his last night's guest. A pile of logs lay between me and the fire, on the top log of which an axe was sticking; and suddenly I discovered that I had some ability at jumping, for in about one and one-half seconds

I was beside Spray—with the axe instead of the pie in my hands—and we, being otherwise unarmed, were figuring out a line of retreat should she ignore the fire and press the matter further. But her charge had been merely to protect her interests at the refuse pile, and as long as we remained on our side of the fire she kept her distance—a distance that would have been more comfortable had it been greater. The moment we attempted to pass around her side of the tent, however, up she came again, repeating her former tactics with perhaps a little more fervor than before. So we took the back way to the foreman's tent, and gave the testimony that was to bring down the death sentence upon her head.

Up from the outpost the next day came two troopers, literally "loaded for bear" with a Krag-Jorgensen carbine, the usual Colt revolvers and, in addition, a Luger automatic pistol—a fast and terrible weapon. With such artillery as this it looked bad indeed for the bears, and we waited the coming of darkness with great interest.

Supper over, every man in the mess tent made for the scene of the last night's encounter to "see the fun;" but such an audience would surely have prevented the results for which we were seeking, as Bruin would have held aloof. As it was, even after we had succeeded in reducing the immediate audience to a half-dozen, no bears appeared. It almost seemed as though they had got wind of our intentions. As nothing had occurred up to nine o'clock we adjourned pro tem to a warm tent, leaving the trooper with the carbine, a big blond corporal, on guard beside the fire.

Perhaps a half-hour had elapsed when three shots rang out in rapid succession from the hollow, causing a rush to the scene from all parts of the camp. We found the big corporal laughing like a boy and declaring that he had "let moonlight into her that time." She had tried upon him the same tactics that she had followed on the preceding evening, but had met with a different response. A bullet from a Krag-Jorgensen rifle is a convincing argument.

But now, where was our bear? If he had hit her fairly her death was certain, but a bear—particularly a silvertip—has tremendous vitality, and it was a question, if she had been hit, how far she would travel before dropping. Darkness forbade any attempt to search that night; but at daylight the next morning a handful of us, including our trooper guests, started out, struck a trail in which were spots of blood in the light snow and walked at least three miles toward the Grand Cañon before deciding that the corporal's bullet had only scratched her back and failed to bring her down.

We returned to camp hungry and disappointed, to find that the laugh was on us; for not two hundred feet across the creek from the scene of the shooting lay our silvertip, a gaping wound in her side bearing terrible witness to the accuracy of one of the corporal's shots. One of the other two shots had evidently struck the foot of another bear not on the program, and it was his trail that we had followed.

The corporal promptly removed the pelt of his quarry, preëmpted by orders from Fort Yellowstone, and with it securely lashed behind the saddle of one of the horses, our trooper friends took their departure. During the ensuing week many of our men made themselves ill over bear meat, too rich in contrast with the routine camp fare to which they had been accustomed; and Dad incidentally built up a flourishing trade in bear grease.

We had no further trouble with bear foragers after that night. If they visited us at all it was surreptitiously, and they were satisfied with eating what could be found at a safe distance from the cook's headquarters. As for Dad, he swore eternal gratitude to the entire United States army for his deliverance from further worry.

1913

The Grizzly and the Can
Ernest Thompson Seton

Besides his *Biography of a Grizzly,* Seton wrote about Yellowstone bears in a few other books. This little account, published in 1913, illustrated one of the complications that arose when bears had easy access to garbage.

The garbage dumps allowed many bears to grow fat and get much larger than they would have eating natural foods. It is an oversimplification to just say that eating garbage was "bad" for bears. It made them less effective at eating natural foods, and it may have been a tragic compromise of the higher purposes of national parks, but it did grow very big bears. We have no way of knowing what all it may have done to harm them, anyway; bears ate a fair amount of junk, including metal and glass, and some got themselves into problems, like this grizzly with the can. But the real trouble of the dumps, at least from a historical perspective, may have been in how they altered the habits of wild animals and how they lessened our opportunities to enjoy those wild animals on their own terms.

When one remembers the Grizzly Bear as the monarch of the mountains, the king of the plains, and the one of matchless might and unquestioned sway among the wild things of the West, it gives one a shock to think of him being conquered and cowed by a little tin can. Yet he was, and this is how it came about.

Cans were a frequent hazard for Yellowstone bears. This black bear was photographed contending with a can in 1938. National Park Service photo.

A grand old Grizzly, that was among the summer retinue of a Park hotel, was working with two claws to get out the very last morsel of some exceptionally delicious canned stuff. The can was extra strong, its ragged edges were turned in, and presently both toes of the Bear were wedged firmly in the clutch of that impossible, horrid little tin trap. The monster shook his paw, and battered the enemy, but it was as sharp within as it was smooth without, and it gripped his paw with the fell clutch of a disease. His toes began to swell with all this effort and violence, till they filled the inner space completely. The trouble was made worse and the paw became painfully inflamed.

All day long that old Grizzly was heard clumping around with that dreadful little tin pot wedged on his foot. Sometimes there was a loud succession of *clamp, clamp, clamp's* which told that the enraged monarch with canned toes was venting his rage on some of the neighboring Black bears.

The next day and the next that shiny tin maintained its frightful grip on the Grizzly, who, limping noisily around, was known and recognized as "Can-foot." His comings and goings to and from the garbage heap, by day and by night, were plainly announced to all by the clamp, clamp, clamp of that maddening, galling tin. Some weeks went by and still the implacable meat box held on.

The officer in charge of the Park came riding by one day; he heard the strange tale of trouble, and saw with his own eyes the limping Grizzly, with his muzzled foot. At a wave of his hand two of the trusty scouts of the Park patrol set out with their ponies and whistling lassoes on the strangest errand that they, or any of their kind, had ever known. In a few minutes those wonderful raw-hide ropes had seized him and the monarch of the mountains was a prisoner bound. Strong shears were at hand. That vicious little can was ripped open. It was completely filled now with the swollen toes. The surgeon dressed the wounds, and the Grizzly was set free. His first blind animal impulse was to attack his seeming tormenters, but they were wise and the ponies were bear-broken; they easily avoided the charge, and he hastened to the woods to recover, finally, both his health and his good temper, and continue about the Park, the only full-grown Grizzly Bear, probably, that man ever captured to help in time of trouble, and then set loose again to live his life in peace.

1913

Midnight Sallies
and Outrageous Nuisances
Jesse L. Smith and W. S. Franklin

Here are two extreme opinions on the "bear problem" that existed in Yellowstone by 1913. Smith thought it was all good fun, and Franklin wanted to kill the bears off. Even back then, Yellowstone's bears could generate a lot of heat in human conversations.

Franklin's story of a man killed in the park while protecting his food seems to be one of those rumors that often run through campgrounds; no such fatality is documented. But Franklin was not uncommon, even in 1913, in his belief that bears were "vermin." It has been a long hard road for the bear from the days when it was considered only a pest and a nuisance to its present position as a symbol of wild country.

To the Editor of Science: In a letter relating to Yellowstone Park which appeared in the issue of SCIENCE for March 21, 1913, there were some statements concerning the experiences which tourists camping out in the park ("sage-brushers," they are usually called) have with the bears, which are certainly astonishing to those who can speak for the sagebrushers if not for the bears. The "cleaning out of sagebrushers' camps by marauding bears" was spoken of as a "nightly occurrence" and it was stated that "three or four sagebrushers are killed nearly every summer in attempting to drive bears out of their camps." My experience as a sagebrusher is that bears will indeed attack the vulnerable part of the camp—the locker containing the store of bacon and the lard can—but even in the vicinity of the Canyon of the Yellowstone, where bears are most numerous, the repelling of an attack on the larder took on much the nature of a midnight sally to rout the neighbor's cow from one's garden patch. There was the same spontaneous rallying against the invasion, the violent laying about with whips and clubs, the resort to loud and picturesque language, and the same clumsy and precipitate retreat of the culprit. Once only we thought it necessary to resort to extreme measures which was to play upon the invaders with a Roman candle. This was completely effective. I would not have a single person miss the great fun and superior advantage of camping out during the tour of the park because of the fear of the bears.

The bears were, truly, everywhere. Near Tower Falls, 1930. National Park Service photo.

A statement from Lieutenant Colonel L. M. Brett, acting super-intendent of the park, under date of April 5, 1913, should certainly reassure all who contemplate a camping trip. I quote as follows:

> As a matter of fact, no tourist or other person has ever been killed by a bear in the park, so far as is known in this office. Our regulations prohibit feeding or meddling with bears, but it is a great temptation for every one to feed them and make pets of them, and the regulations are sometimes violated. Otherwise, there would seldom be any bad bears in the park. As it is, we have instances where the bear becomes dangerous to life and property, and it is necessary to dispense of it. This is done by capture alive and shipment by express to some city zoo, when there is a demand for a bear, and in case there is no demand for it, it is shot. A few instances are on record where people have been attacked and injured by bears. One of these was a tourist; the others were employees of hotels, etc., in the park. In all cases where the facts were known, the person injured was more or less to blame for his own misfortune.

To the Editor of Science: I have tramped, with knapsack and sleeping bag, more than a thousand miles through the wildest and roughest parts of the Rocky Mountains, camping out in the cheapest and most primitive fashion; and every one will understand, I think, that it is not as a molly-coddle that I say, from my experience during the summer of 1911, that the bear in Yellowstone Park are an outrageous nuisance.

I know of no more flagrant example of detached, red-taped sophistry than this: "A few instances are on record where people have been attacked and injured by bears" but "in all cases where the facts were known the person injured was more or less to blame."[1] In speaking of this as detached I mean that it must have been written either with little knowledge or scant appreciation of the facts.

During the summer of 1911 I traveled with three boys about 300 miles through the country south and southeast of Yellowstone Park, and one night a man who had been turned away from the Reclamation Camp at Jackson Lake was seen prowling around our wagon, which was at some distance from the tent where we were sleeping. A little biggity talk about guns and shooting was enough to scare

---

[1] See letter of Jesse L. Smith in SCIENCE of June 20.

the poor fellow away, but if he could not have been scared away he would certainly have gotten a dose of lead.

When we got into the Yellowstone Park we pitched our tent in a good place and proceeded to take in the wonderful sights; but we were warned by a soldier that we must stand guard over our camp after dusk or we would be cleaned out by marauding bear. How would you, curious reader, like to be tied down to guard duty over a side of bacon in Yellowstone Park? We went there for another purpose; but we remembered that we were a long way from a base of supplies!

Our first night in the park we slept with an axe under our pillow, thinking to drive Mr. Bear out of our pantry if he should come in the night; which is precisely the most foolish thing we could have done, Mr. Jesse L. Smith to the contrary notwithstanding. If Mr. Bear should happen to be Mrs. Bear with a cub it would be pretty dangerous business. One of the killings (man killings) we heard of during the summer of 1911 was a three-cornered affair or rather a three-in-a-row affair of this kind, and the man was unfortunately in the middle. Quoting from the park superintendent we would say that this man "was more or less to blame." At any rate we must admit that he was thinking too much of his stock of grub and of his remoteness from a base of supplies. But we would not have been blameworthy if we had shot the poor hobo from Jackson Lake. No, before God, we wouldn't.

Mr. Jesse L. Smith's reference to the frightening of bear with Roman candles reminds me of the crank who proposed to squirt olive oil and phosphorus over the Bastile to set it on fire at the beginning of the French Revolution. Phosphorus was only a chemical curiosity on those days, and probably all that had ever been made would have amounted to less than a pound, and it is extremely amusing to read Carlyle's exhortation to this visionary crank to bring forth his phosphorus and olive oil! The unfortunate but blameworthy man above referenced to ought to have had sense enough to have used a Roman candle, or, better still, a hand grenade filled with liquid anhydrous ammonia! He showed his respect for law, however, in not using a bomb containing liquefied prussic acid; that would have killed the bear.

We lost all of our grub at the Canyon, and we ate at the hotels during the remainder of our trip; a very pleasant change after eight weeks of rough and tumble camping, but extravagantly expensive from a teacher's point of view. We knew directly of several small camps besides our own that were raided during our five or six days in the park. Greenhorns, Mr. Smith would say. Yes, they were greenhorns in the park under the fatherly care of the superintendent and his company of cavalry; but it would not have been healthy for man or beast to have gone very far on that assumption outside of the park.

We heard incessant talk about marauding bears; just as we hear incessant talk about the weather in Kansas, without fear, but with deep concern. And we heard circumstantial accounts of at least two campers who were seriously hurt in trying to save their grub. Their midnight sallies were not like "routing a neighbor's cow from a garden patch," to quote Mr. Smith.

The simple fact is that either ninety-five per cent of the Yellowstone Park bears must be killed off or soldiers must be placed on all-night guard around the chief camping places in the park. Mr. Smith, and to some extent also the park superintendent, make themselves ridiculous in looking at this matter in the spirit of complacent statisticians unmindful of the cold fact that the exceptional cases are absolutely not to be tolerated.

"I would not have a single person," says Mr. Smith, "miss the great fun and superior advantage of camping out during the tour of the park because of the fear of the bears." Mr. Smith is pedantic in his choice of words. It is purely a question of vermin. And Mr. Smith, who boldly routs marauding bear with Roman candles, perhaps, if properly armed, he would not be afraid even of a bed bug.

1919

Holdup Bears
Horace Albright

Local folklore has long held that the first roadside beggar bear in Yellow-stone appeared a year or two after automobiles were allowed to enter the park in 1915. According to this tradition, a black bear cub, quickly named Jesse James, learned to beg at the road near West Thumb.

Actually, a variety of historical sources suggest that roadside begging started back closer to 1900, intermittently here and there in the park. But it wasn't until about 1918 or 1919 that beggar bears became a major visitor attraction. In the following brief report on Yellowstone bears, taken from the 1919 *Annual Report of the Director of the National Park Service,* Horace Albright (then Yellowstone superintendent) tells of visitor persistence in feeding bears.

Bear-feeding regulations were rarely enforced before the late 1960s, and so roadside bear feeding, like the garbage dump feedground, became a Yellowstone institution, and no traffic problem was more common in the park than the great "bear jams," where dozens of cars would be backed up, waiting their turn to photograph the bear and toss it some junk food.

The grizzly, black, and brown bears were plentiful and much in evidence throughout the park and attracted so much attention and were so much talked about that the few tourists who failed to see them felt disappointed. These bears were so mischievous that it was neces-

Park Superintendent Horace Albright, 1922.

sary to keep a night guard at Upper Basin, Lake Outlet, and Canyon to prevent damage to private automobiles and campms, and five had to be killed at Lake during the summer to prevent damage to property. One medium-sized grizzly was killed in September at Upper Geyser Basin in a fight with a larger grizzly.

In addition to the bears that made a habit of frequenting the regular camping places, garbage dumps were established within walking distance of Upper Basin and Canyon, where bears of all kinds congregated every evening just before dark, and it was a regular practice for people from the hotels and campms to go to see them. A wire was firmly stretched between trees and posts to keep people from going beyond the danger line, and a ranger was placed on duty with a rifle to protect them. This is one of the most interesting features of the park to the majority of tourists, but requires careful regulation.

But even more interesting than the bear dumps were a few clever bears, among them one or two families consisting of mother and cubs, that frequented the highway between Thumb and Lake Outlet and daily "held up" passing automobiles and begged for food. As a rule the tourists so held up were willing victims of the robbers, and most of them would risk being tried before the United States commissioner for violation of park regulations, which prohibit "approaching, molesting, or feeding the bears," rather than turn a deaf ear to the appeals of the cubs for candy, peanuts, etc. This rule is the most difficult to enforce of all the park rules and regulations, as indicated by the fact that of 28 trials before the United States court during the past summer for violation of regulations not one was for this offense.

1920s

The Lady Who Lost Her Dress
Horace Albright

By the 1920s, bear bites were perhaps a more serious matter than Mr. Albright might have thought, if only because they were a preview of the increased number of injuries that would occur in the 1930s. Mr. Albright was right, in any case, that most injuries were minor and that quite a few of these close encounters would play quite well with the neighbors when the visitor got back home.

Next to the geysers (and possibly illegal hooch), the bears gave park visitors the most pleasure—and they still do. From the time tourist facilities were put into operation back in 1883, and perhaps earlier, garbage from hotels and camps was deposited about a mile from the kitchens. Thousands of people visited these piles to watch the antics of the black bears, coyotes, gulls, and, as twilight faded into darkness, grizzly bears. Near Old Faithful geyser, in the Upper Geyser Basin, and at the Yellowstone Canyon, I had "Greek theaters" built of logs, and there hundreds of park visitors went to watch the animals. A mounted ranger, with a rifle at the ready, was stationed between the seated visitors and the bears, to protect both.

Along the roads, black bears here and there waited for passing cars to stop and throw out food. They also raided camps at night if food was left within reach. They were called "beggar bears" or "hold-up bears," and were harmless unless provoked. Sometimes hands would be held out to get the bear to rise on his hind legs for photographs—when no food was in the extended hand. Then the bear sometimes bit. When a tourist made a complaint about a finger bite, I would advise him, first, that he should not have fed the bear; second, that the wound was superficial, and finally, that really it was a unique souvenir to take home. This observation rarely failed to convince the visitor that he really had something worthwhile, though I never heard of one going back for another.

One day, a lady telephoned from Canyon Lodge. She wanted a black bear "killed at once." She said no one had ever been hurt or humiliated as she had been. I sent a ranger to investigate. He reported that she had been feeding a big bear all morning, and tourists had been photographing the two of them. She had enticed the bear to the lodge platform just as several hundred people were boarding buses after lunch. The bear stood up as she fed him from her fingers. Passengers in and out of the buses were taking pictures when somebody distracted her. The bear, thinking the show was over, dropped to the ground, but, in so doing, caught his claws in the shoulder straps of her dress, stripping her before the throng. She admitted to the ranger that she had not been physically injured, but none of us doubted that she had been terribly humiliated. We spared the bear, however.

Close Contact with Grizzly Bears
Phillip Martindale

As Horace Albright explained in the previous story, many rangers spent part of their summer on dump duty. For some this involved only keeping watch, armed with a shotgun, in case some bear should approach the crowd too closely (this seems to have been a pretty rare occurrence). A few rangers became teachers, providing commentary on the doings of the bears that fed on the garbage.

One of the best known of these rangers was Phillip Martindale, who held forth many nights in the 1920s, sitting astride his horse only yards from the bears. His brief reminiscence is an impressive testimonial to the temperament of his horse.

It is unlikely that Mr. Martindale saw very many "900 lb." grizzly bears. That is an extremely large – though by no means impossible, especially in the dump days – bear for Yellowstone.

The bear feeding grounds lecture stadium at Old Faithful seats now about 2,700 people and is usually crowded at the 7 o'clock lecture on wild animals. Most always certain loud noises, laughter, hand-clapping, etc., prevail during the lecture.

Phillip Martindale and his brave horse during an evening bear talk at the Old Faithful feeding grounds in the 1920s. National Park Service photo.

It is only about 125 feet from the crowd behind the cable to the lunch counter or platform where the food is placed to attract the bears, and the horse (as a lecture platform) is backed up to within 30 feet of the platform, which in turn is only about 50 feet from the woods.

Training and confidence are responsible for the fact that the horse will not even turn when a grizzly comes in behind him, but this has taken time and patience. However, the grizzly bear, truly a wild animal, now comes out without hesitation majestically in daylight to the counter, the lecture and attendant noises not in the least distracting him, with all the great audience in mass directly in front of him.

It has taken four years to accomplish this and they all seem to know the sound of my voice and do not wait in the timber, as in previous years, until dark.

It is understood that a young immature grizzly will at times foolishly take chances that his elders do not, so we see cases of the

The bear-feeding stand at the Old Faithful feeding grounds, 1929. National Park Service photo.

An audience at the Old Faithful feeding grounds in 1929, held spellbound by the show. National Park Service photo.

youngster breaking certain bear rules, but to have the 900 lb. bear come in under the above circumstances at this point makes us feel proud of the protective confidence finally gained. This has only been in progress since July.

On a certain night early in August a grizzly came around the pit by mistake and came directly toward my horse, within 15 feet, in fact. I waited for him to turn but finally and quickly decided that he did not see me. I made a noise and sudden motion, which caused him to stand up on his hind legs and then he turned. Their eyesight is unquestionably dull living as they do in deep timber.

We recently constructed an additional feeding counter adjoining the other one, so that more bears could feed at once—also we now feed them directly before the lecture starts and have practically dispelled the idea that full grown blacks and grizzlies will not eat close together. It now is found possible to have not only the youngsters but large bears quiet on the lunch counter at the same time.

The effect of this close contact to an animal that is considered the greatest of all wild North American carnivores, showing what real protection can do, is good. The public carry it away in their minds.

1924

Grizzly Visits
Snowshoe Cabin
E. J. Sawyer

The cavalry established a system of tiny backcountry cabins for use of their soldiers while they were watching for poachers. These were called "snowshoe cabins" because they were most used by soldiers in winter, when most park travel was accomplished by snowshoes (in those days the term *snowshoes* was usually used to mean skis). The National Park Service kept this system of cabins in place and now calls them patrol cabins. They are sturdily built, for the most part, and give one a feeling of security—unless one has read a few accounts like the following.

On approaching the snowshoe cabin on Upper Pelican Creek I met Ranger Dunrud coming from the cabin where he had spent the night. Following is the substance of Mr. Dunrud's account of the condition in which he found the cabin on his arrival the day before. The door had been opened by main force. The bedding, including the mattress, had been all taken outside and strewn on the snow for distances varying up to 100 feet. The bed itself (a large heavily built affair) had been moved two feet out from the wall; the stove had been moved from its place, the zinc-covered cupboard had been turned over, broken into and contents emptied, provisions all eaten or (such as pepper and cinnamon) at least bitten into, excepting one small especially resistant tin. Every frying pan, dish pan and kettle had been knocked from the walls. A sack of oats had been torn from its nail on the ceiling, and contents eaten.

The tracks alone of a single enormous grizzly bear coming to and leaving the cabin left no doubt of the visitor's identity. Mr. Dunrud had put the cabin in shipshape again, but I can personally testify to the tracks of the grizzly in the snow; I followed them for a mile both ways from the cabin.

1925

Tracking an Old Grizzly
Milton Skinner

Following a bear, even a short distance, is an exercise in head-turning. Like the bear ahead of you, you must be looking in all directions. As you follow, you will see where it turned over a few rocks here, dug tentatively for a bulb or root there, or checked out a marmot den here, never stopping its open-minded shopping trip.

I don't know what year Skinner made this little excursion, so I have assigned it to the year his book *Bears in the Yellowstone* was published. Whenever it was, the bear gave him a good lesson in creative wandering.

I know of nothing that gives one a better idea of bear sagacity and cunning, as well as individuality, than to trail up an old grizzly, wise in his years of discretion. To trail such a big animal by his tracks in the snow seems a simple task. And so it would be if it were not the track of a resourceful, intelligent animal with limb and wind sufficient to carry him anywhere he may elect to go. Old Eph cannot be treed, and he will not travel in circles, or follow any other rule that gives one a chance to forestall or get ahead of him. Grizzlies that are followed use their brains all the time and apparently never become panic-stricken. They can travel the roughest of rocky, mountainous regions with surprising agility and speed. And, furthermore, the following of a trail and working out its tangles, its turns, its counter-turns, and its various eccentricities is a liberal education for the trailer. He who matches himself against this past master of woodcraft, he who pits his skill, his care, and his endurance against the grizzly, will learn much, will acquire much new respect, for bruin. And in the learning will enjoy much in the way of entertainment and satisfaction.

When I was but a boy in college, I began hunting the grizzly. I learned a great deal of him, of his ways and habits, of his courage and sagacity; and I learned to respect his sturdy qualities. I perse-vered, at times I was successful—more often I was not. I steadily acquired woodcraft; I often returned to camp dirty, wet, and tired out, but I never regretted those days in the forest. As for the grizzly, I began by respecting him and then I came to admire him. For many years now I have not used a rifle; sometimes I take a camera, but more often I spend days studying the great bear, and still my wonder and respect increases the more I learn. I have found that the trailing of Old Eph, wise and wary in his old age, is the most difficult, the most exhaustive of all wildwood tests.

One autumn when the snow fell just right and lay two or three inches deep for five days without melting, or crusting so as to be noisy, I took a blanket, a little food, a light pack, and a camera to track down a grizzly. I found his trail in a small meadow where the remains of a squirrel burrow still covered the snow with fresh dirt and the long grass was still rising from bruin's footsteps in a way to indicate only two or three hours' start. He was not traveling fast and I had high hopes of catching up. Soon after I started I noticed that most of the time he traveled into the face of the wind. This, of course, was to be informed of what was in front of him as far as possible. In a way this made my work lighter, for any noise I made could not so readily reach those keen ears and no telltale scent could give me away. But Old Eph knew that as well as I did ad it made him still more watchful of his rear; in fact, he apparently never felt safe about his back track and was always alert to possible approach from that direction. As the day wore on, the snow told me that he frequently stopped and rose on his haunches to look and listen and probably to sniff in all directions. Since the snow was fairly well melted in such places from the heat of the body, it was evident he spent many minutes in each survey, although I was quite sure it was not until two days later that he felt he was being followed. If these ordinary investigations did not fully satisfy him, he made a slow circle, stopping whenever he saw something he wanted, but, nevertheless, eventually getting back across his trail before going on again. Once or twice during the day he back-tracked along his trail, possibly to see if all was well. He did not by any means travel straight away, nor even in any general direction. He was unalarmed, he was attending to his ordinary business of securing enough to eat; he cropped grass, he dug mice, squirrels, and woodchucks, he tore up logs, and he over-turned many stones. But, as a grizzly habitually does, he watched his back track to prevent surprise.

On a small plateau where almost every stone was turned, he crossed and recrossed his own trail so repeatedly I could not follow its tortuous ways, and only by making a big circle myself could I pick up the onward trail again. At times he climbed a rock or a hillside to look back, and again he turned at right angles to his trail for a sufficient distance to have sound or scent come from his back trail. He used a number of methods to deceive anyone that might be on his trail, so that I could not foretell what was coming next. Some-times he went straight across an open meadow or "park" only to "stop, look, and listen" in the far edge of the woods; sometimes he passed around the opening to the left, sometimes to the right; and once or twice he right-angled in the middle of a meadow and went out to one side.

Although years of trailing and tracking had long since raised me out of the novice class, I could not foresee and anticipate his move-ments, and I had to risk his seeing me in the openings, or else lose time circling to pick up his trail again. On the third day his trail started diagonally down a canyon wall and I assumed he was going to the bottom, and accordingly let myself down over an easier course than his, to the creek. Failing to cross and pick up the trail there, I was obliged to climb back. There I found the bear had gone two-thirds of the way down, then turned sharply and climbed to a shelf and bedded down for several hours. Afterward he climbed to the ridge, went back a mile, recrossing his old trail, then down to the creek bottom, and, turning away from his previous course, climbed to the far ridge and on again. But now he seemed to be aware I was following, and I believe he had seen me in the gulch, for I crossed the creek so soon after him that his tracks still contained muddy water. I followed him two days longer, but he did not vary his tactics at all except to travel fast enough to keep ahead. I actually saw him twice during the last two days, neither time within rifle shot, and still more hopeless for my camera. At no point did I outwit him completely, and he defeated most of the plans I made to cut across on his trail and forestall him; yet he did not seem to eat less than usual or to hurry to any extent.

1927

Ranger Treed by Grizzly
E. J. Sawyer

Park visitors weren't always the source of bear stories. Life in grizzly bear country guaranteed the occasional close call, and more than one park employee has spent some uncomfortable hours in a tree waiting for a bear to leave. There is even a wonderful, if undocumented, local tale of a ranger, out on a winter ski trip, who encountered a grizzly out of its den. The ranger, so the story goes, climbed a tree, realizing after he was safely in its branches that he hadn't even taken his skis off.

Ranger Ogsten was lucky. Don't ever try to outrun a grizzly bear. No action is guaranteed to protect you, but most experts agree that unless a good tree is very close, your best bet is to play dead.

The following incident occurred about one mile from the Yellowstone Canyon on the road to Norris. Ranger Ted Ogsten was walking down the road when he heard something approaching from the front. Owing to the darkness, for it was 11:00 P.M., he was at first unable to make anything out; but, soon he discovered a grizzly bear accompanied by her two cubs. When Ogsten stopped to pick up stones with which to frighten the bears away he says he could hear the mother scratching on the ground; then she growled and made a forward spurt, with one cub on each side. Ogsten turned and ran over a hundred yards before, seeing that the bears were gaining, he took to the woods beside the road. Finally coming to a tree which he could climb quickly, he was soon above reach of the bears which were then only thirty feet away. The old grizzly and the cubs came near the base of the tree, but they made no further threatening move or sound whatever; they did, however, remain in the neighborhood for at least ten minutes. Unable to determine, in the semi-darkness, as to whether or not his late pursuers had really left the vicinity, the ranger remained in the tree for about an hour. He says the cold had become almost unbearable before he at last ventured down and made for the ranger station. Nothing more was seen of the grizzly family that night.

Mr. Ogsten says he would very much like to know what those grizzlies would have done, had he not retreated. That, indeed, is the question. Nor is it likely that the answer will ever be learned from any man mentally and physically normal as long as the circumstances include a tree of fair size and convenient branches.

1927

Bears Become Bold
E. J. Sawyer

The park's larger developments were no more safe from bears than were the backcountry cabins. It amazes me that more people weren't killed, and I suspect they weren't only because there were so few people around by October, when the following report was written.

After the close of the tourist season, the abundant supply of table scraps from the hotels being at an end, the bears usually become more bold and look to the road camps and woodcutters' camps for a larger part of their rations. During the present fall the bears have been troublesome and high-handed in an extraordinary degree, breaking into camps and stores and greatly disturbing the peace of road crews and others. Two of the Hamilton stores—those at the West Thumb and the Lake, respectively—were broken into and much of the stock was mauled and strewn about with considerable loss and damage. Two of the woodcutters' camps at the Canyon were so infested with bears, especially grizzlies, that regular night guards were kept busy warding away the prowlers by means of Roman candles and other devices. All sorts of adventures are related, attesting to the boldness and persistence of the bears; stories of "narrow escapes" are not

Black bear shopping for lunch, Mammoth Hot Springs, 1928. National Park Service photo.

wanting. The cries of a cub, when the latter was seized by a dog belonging to one of the camps, moved one mother grizzly to chase a man who stumbled and was overtaken. It is still this man's unshaken belief that the sputtering stump of a Roman candle held as a despairing jesture in the very face of the bear, was the only thing that saved him from painful and bloody deaath. As many as fourteen bears, together with an undetermined number of cubs, were seen at one time about a given camp. Finally, an iron cage-trap was set at the Canyon bear feeding ground and a female grizzly was soon caught. A large delegation of grizzlies visited the captive and seemed to try to free her. Two or three days later every grizzly except the prisoner had disappeared completely from the region; nor, as yet, have any of them returned. The captive is to be shipped to the zoo in the city of Denver.

1929

Bear Steals U.S. Mail
Dorr G. Yeager

Was nothing sacred?

Everyone is acquainted with the "hold-up" bears in Yellowstone Park, and nearly everyone has, at one time or another, experienced the sensation of being held up by one of these forest clowns. A new phase of this unlawful business came to my attention a few days ago, however, when Dick White related the following story of his experience at West Thumb.

It seems that some days ago Dick stopped at the West Thumb road camp for lunch. The season being closed, and the regular mail delivery having ceased, Dick was obligingly carrying a bundle of mail with him for the members of the different road crews around the loop. He left the mail in the car and, after enjoying a good meal, returned to continue his journey to Lake. Imagine his surprise, however, to find the package of mail not in the car but between the paws of a black bear in a nearby tree. Bruin was examining the packet intently, sniffing and turning it over in an inquisitive manner. Suddenly he began to tear at it and, disregarding the shouts and threats of the man below, continued until he had extracted a box from its contents. The tree was shaken, clubs and threats were hurled but the bear, utterly unmindful of the commotion he was causing, tore open the box and feasted happily on the contents, which proved to be chocolates. Having emptied the box thoroughly, licked his paws, and minutely inspected the remainder of the mail for further delicacies he reluctantly dropped it into the arms of the waiting man below, and with a contented grunt settled himself down on the limb until such a time as his tormentor should retire.

1937

Five Too Many Grizzlies
Marguerite Lindsley Arnold

What may be most notable about this incident, however exciting the bear's charge may have been for Mrs. Arnold, is that there are very few reported cases of grizzly sows with four cubs in Yellowstone.

Late in the evening of October 31 while driving from Mammoth to Cooke Ranger Station with Mrs. Pierson and my son, Billy, we had an exciting encounter with grizzlies.

We had crossed the Gardiner River Bridge, two miles out from Mammoth, and started the climb up the hill. As our car lights swept around the curve they revealed five grizzlies in the road. We stopped the car at once and saw that it was a mother and four yearling cubs. After a quick survey, the bears turned and ran up the road.

Anxious to see how fast they were traveling, we followed. Two of the cubs were successful in clamboring up the hillside but the others continued up the snow-covered highway.

The mother suddenly stopped, reared to watch the car lights, and then charged! Either the lights seemed too ominous, even to a grizzly, or she changed her mind for with equal abruptness she stopped, altogether too close, and raced back after her cubs. Once

A busload of visitors in a typical "holdup." Photos like these were important promotional devices for attracting visitors to the park. The cost—in human injuries and bears destroyed because they became too dangerous—was high, but even this early, bear feeding was an institution that could not easily be controlled.

more we followed. Again that huge beast turned and charged. She approached us, as grizzlies do, on a double-time lope. As she had stopped before, we naturally expected—at least hoped—that she would act accordingly this time. But . . . on she came. It was snowing lightly, and what a picture that bear made as she rushed upon us! Providentially, she slid to a stop when within a foot of the car, sniffed, blinked at the lights, and retreated once more.

This bear may not have been very large, but when standing on four feet, the roach of her back came up even with the top of the radiator of our Hudson.

Resuming the chase up the long grade, we found that the best speed of the bears was fifteen miles per hour.

1939

Bears Behind Bars
William Rush

William Rush was a biologist who spent several years studying wildlife in the Yellowstone area. By his time, bear-handling was a routine part of a ranger's work. But it was by no means humdrum work, and many a trapping session did not go as planned. It's still that way.

"What kind of a rifle shall we take along?" asked Ranger Hanks.

"None," said Ranger Trischman in positive tones. "If we have a gun with us we're sure to get into trouble."

They were getting ready to go to the Canyon bear feeding grounds to capture some grizzly bears alive for zoological gardens in Salt Lake City, Cleveland, Philadelphia, and Pittsburgh. Orders had been verified, permission granted by the government, shipping crates built, receiving pens were ready at the zoos; everything was done except catching the bears, and Harry Trischman, the most experienced and level-headed ranger in the whole Park Service, was detailed for the job.

It was October and most black bears had gone, either in search of food elsewhere or to their winter dens. Grizzlies were not as plentiful as they had been during the summer, but there were still a few around road camps and hotels. Bears were cross and dangerous at

Even the coal bucket was worth a look. No location is recorded for this 1929 Yellowstone photograph. National Park Service photo.

this time of year. The liberal quantities of food they had been getting from hotels were diminished in August and had been cut off entirely in September. Bears kept returning to the feeding grounds just the same, hoping for more free handouts, and when these were not forthcoming they got mean. They seemed to realize the gravity of their plight, going into hibernation hungry when they should have been fat for their long winter sleep, and they were ready to fight about it with anyone at any time.

Trapping grizzlies is always interesting and this expedition promised unusual excitement, so I was ready to go when Hanks and

Trischman hitched their bear trap behind a light Ford truck and proceeded to Canyon, armed only with pick handles for protection.

The bear trap was a huge cage, constructed of steel plates and rods, mounted on an automobile chassis. One end was made of steel bars a half-inch in diameter, welded into the frame and strengthened by two crossbars. The other end was a solid steel door which dropped down into slots when the trigger was sprung inside. The sides were solid steel. A special hitch was arranged so that a truck could back up to the trap and allow a man standing in the truck bed to hook onto it without getting down. This was essential when cubs were caught. The mother always stayed near and was not a particularly pleasant creature to deal with while her cubs were being stolen. The trap was set on the feeding grounds and baited with a large, smelly, greasy bacon rind.

The day was warm and peaceful and everything was quiet in the park with the hordes of tourists gone. The only sound that broke the silence was pounding of hammers at the hotel where carpenters were busy nailing up doors and windows, making things secure for the long eight months of winter. They were a half-mile away and the sound came to us as a subdued tattoo which emphasized rather than disturbed the stillness as we went about our task of preparing the trap.

Harry was sure we'd have a bear by morning.

"Maybe two of 'em," he said hopefully that night at the ranger station. "Better roll in early so's we can get there first thing in the morning, before they hurt themselves too much!"

It was storming when we awoke. A cold wind howled across the yard and snow blew into our faces as we hurried out to the truck.

"A little taste of the winter that's coming," Harry said as we drove along the road toward Canyon.

We caught a glimpse of the trap as we came around the turn a quarter of a mile away from it. The door was down. We had something!

"Hope it's that pair of cubs we're after," said Harry, stepping a little harder on the accelerator.

I jumped out of the truck before it stopped rolling and hurried over to look through the bars at the end of the cage. At the sight that met my eyes I let out a yell that brought Harry running to my side.

"What is it?" he asked wonderingly.

A piteous moan came from a crumpled heap of clothing at the other end of the cage and a face, blue with cold, was turned toward us.

"It's the hotel cook!" Harry exclaimed. "Here—let's get him out of there!"

We hurried to raise the heavy door and rescue the poor man who was almost frozen and literally paralyzed with fright. It took us quite a while to get his story, but after we had thawed him out in front of his own kitchen fire he managed to tell us what had happened.

"The weather was so nice yesterday, and I didn't have anything to do but cook for those carpenters, so along in the afternoon I decided to go for a walk. I didn't take a coat—." He shivered and drew the blanket more tightly around him. "Just went out in my kitchen clothes and wandered toward the old dump. I'd seen you fellows down there earlier and wanted to see what you'd been doing."

Harry grinned. "Too bad you didn't come a little sooner. We could'a saved you some trouble."

"Yeah," the cook grinned back, feebly. "But when I got down there you were gone and I went inside to see how the big cage looked. There was some kind of a contraption at the far end. I wanted to find out what it was.

"I found out, all right. I just barely touched that bacon rind when the big door went clang! behind me. There I was, and I knew I couldn't get out, even before I'd tried every way I knew to lift that door.

"I yelled for help—thought sure that when the carpenters went in to supper and didn't find me they'd come out and look, so I kept yelling every few minutes until I was so hoarse I could hardly speak above a whisper.

"Then bears began to come. It was awful! They tried to get at me through the bars and when they couldn't reach me with their claws they rocked the cage back and forth and tried to turn it over. Two of the biggest grizzlies began to fight and made the most awful noises I ever heard in my life. I hope I'm never near another grizzly fight. They came up and looked at me through the bars and I could see their white teeth gleaming in the dark and feel their hot breath. They smelled hot, too—hot and bloody and dirty.

"When I got a chance I poked the bacon rind out through the

bars, thinking it might satisfy them. They got into an awful fight over it—ten of them—fighting over that rind for a good half-hour. Their growls and snarls made my blood run cold. After the fight they all came back and two or three of the biggest ones got on top of the cage and tried to break in that way. I thought I was a goner sure, but the cage was too strong for them. Even the biggest ones couldn't dent it."

Harry said, "I never thought of it that way before, but if it's strong enough to keep one of them in, I guess it'll keep 'em out, too."

The cook wrapped the blanket around him and shivered again.

"Then it began to get cold. It must have been zero last night. I never was so cold in my life and I thought morning would never come. What time did you boys get there?"

"Right after breakfast," Harry said. "We ate that before daylight. You couldn't 'a been in there over fifteen hours, could he, Bill?"

"Long enough!" I exclaimed and laughed in spite of myself. I'd have bet my bottom dollar that here was one man who'd never crawl into another bear trap, much less spring the trigger.

We walked out of the hotel and Harry stopped to talk to one of the carpenters.

"Weren't you worried when the cook didn't show up last night?" I asked another workman.

"Oh, not specially," the man said slowly. "We figgered he'd turn up this mornin'—but if he hadn't been here by dinner time today we'd 'a gone lookin' fer him."

The carpenter said, "We knew he wouldn't get et up by bears because the naturalist said bears won't touch human flesh!"

Harry was chuckling as we walked on and when we were well out of hearing he said wisely, "I don't think he's a very good cook. Probably burns the beans!"

There were still bears to catch and this time the trap was baited with a juicy ham bone. Next morning two cubs were inside and Harry was elated. He had expected to find this the most difficult part of his job, and here he had the pair he wanted the second day. The snow storm had abated somewhat, but the day was cloudy and chilly and the road still slick from snow.

Old Mother Grizzly was waiting when the truck backed down to the trap. She was mad. All night she had been trying to get her

A grizzly bear in its shipping cage in 1941, probably on its way to a zoo. National Park Service photo.

cubs out of that cage and she had worked herself into a frenzy. It took nerve to hook up to the cage and start away with it. There was no way of knowing just what the old girl would do.

She ran after the cage for a little way, but, as the truck gathered speed, she saw that she was hopelessly outrun, so she stopped and seemed to be thinking over the problem. The road curved from the feeding grounds in almost a half-circle to the hotel and then turned sharply toward a high bridge across Cascade Creek. Mother bear hesitated only a few seconds, then started as fast as she could run straight toward the bridge, taking a short cut that gave her a chance to head off the truck that was carrying her cubs away.

About a hundred yards from the bridge Harry saw her coming through the trees.

"Step on it!" he yelled. "She'll get us at the bridge!"

Ranger Hanks' heavy foot pressed the accelerator clear to the floor, but the wheels didn't take hold and the careening vehicle barely won the race. There weren't more than thirty feet to spare when we rolled onto the bridge.

As soon as the old bear saw that her strategy had failed, she turned and disappeared into the forest. No one knows what would have happened if she had been able to get to the bridge first. She might have tackled the outfit, smashed into the cab, and mangled all of us. Luck was with us and the cubs were soon whisked to the railhead, transferred to shipping crates, and loaded on an express car for fast shipment to the eastern United States.

A few nights later an old female was caught. She was an enormous bear with a ferocious temper. When we arrived at the trap she had already broken several teeth and some of her claws in her efforts to break out. As soon as we came within sight her fury was redoubled. She tore at the bars with claws and teeth. She even sat on the floor of the cage with her back against one side and her feet against the other, pushing with all her might. It was a real test for the cage. The old girl put a permanent bulge in its steel plates, but she couldn't break it apart.

She probably had cubs somewhere outside. Most bears became quiet and lay down in the cage as soon as the truck began to roll along the road, but her rage increased when she felt it start. She rushed from one end of the cage to the other, throwing her weight against

Yellowstone bear of unrecorded species being loaded for shipment to Holland; Yellowstone bears stocked many zoos. National Park Service photo.

the bars. The men stopped the car when we had gone about ten miles and found that she had broken all her claws. Her feet were bleeding freely. Her teeth were damaged and her mouth was bleeding, too. The only thing neither bruised or broken was her spirit.

All of us were feeling sorry for her and wishing for a good excuse to turn her loose. Finally Ranger Hanks said, "Well, she's not a very good specimen for a zoo. Teeth and claws are gone."

Harry agreed quickly, "She doesn't look very good. Let's turn her loose and catch another one. I'll get on top of the cage and lift the trap door as soon as you get the truck to rolling."

"O.K.," said Hanks in a relieved tone. He was glad to get rid of this bear and so was I. Her roars would persist in my ears for a long time if they shipped her away.

When the truck had attained a speed of ten or fifteen miles an hour Harry pulled up the heavy steel door. The bear rushed out, tumbled over and over in the road, regained her feet, and started after the truck, gaining at every stride.

"Step on it! Step on it!" Harry yelled. "She's gaining on us!"

The truck seemed to hang motionless for a moment, then it pulled slowly away. The last Harry saw of the bear she was still chasing us. Badly punished physically, deprived of her cubs and with her deeply ingrained dignity outraged, still she had the fighting courage and spirit that are such outstanding qualities of grizzlies.

A few days later Harry was cornered on top of the trap by a mad grizzly. Harry had placed the bacon rind bait inside, arranged the figure-four trip, and climbed on top to adjust the heavy steel drop door when the grizzly rushed him. The top of the trap was plate steel like the sides, about four feet wide by eight feet long and a good six feet above the ground. The bear reared up and hit the trap with terrific force, almost upsetting it. Harry had the weapon he had chosen, a pick handle, and he wielded it with telling effect on that grizzly's nose and head. The bear tried to clamber up there with him. She got so many clouts over the head with the pick handle that she did not succeed. Had there been two grizzlies, one on each side of the trap, Harry would have been out of luck, but he managed to stand this one off.

Although grizzlies are stout-hearted and have plenty of grit, I'd back Harry Trischman against one of them any time. It was a sight to watch—Harry laughing at the grizzly when she reared up to her full height, a good two feet higher than the trap, put her paws on the edge of the cage, and reached for him with mouth open, looking eager to tear him to pieces. There was a quick, precisely timed blow with the pick handle and the bear went down on all fours again. The performance was repeated until at last she gave up, a badly licked, soreheaded, but wiser grizzly.

Back in the truck Ranger Hanks asked, "Didn't you wish for a gun that time, Harry?"

And Harry replied with his customary grin, "Nope! If I'd had a gun I'd have got into trouble with that bear, sure!"

Part Four

THE BEAR STUDENTS

The rangers and naturalists of the National Park Service have always taken a serious interest in bears. Though extended scientific study of Yellowstone's bears did not get underway until 1959, many small, informal studies occurred much earlier. Occasionally a visiting biologist would make some observations and publish the results in a technical journal, but most of the findings appeared less formally, and were far less widely read, in the little newspaper entitled *Yellowstone Nature Notes,* which was produced in small mimeographed editions starting in the early 1920s.

I offer here only a small sampling of this material, which has been all but lost to public view. These selections suggest the intensity and continuity of interest shown by park staff in bears and also suggest the earnest (if slightly innocent) attitude of early park naturalists.

I never tire of this material. These rangers and other park employees were relating their experiences and observations partly to assist each other in educating the public, but perhaps more because it was something they enjoyed doing. Some of their attitudes may surprise us now; they were often quite anthropomorphic when writing of wildlife. But there is a freshness to their little inquiries that sometimes amuses us so much that we don't notice just how much information they were piling up. Seen together, it was a lot; even before 1950, Yellowstone's bears had been the source of substantial amounts of natural history information.

I have divided this section into three parts, each with a general introduction for several selections. Within each part, I've simply organized the selections chronologically. They are not offered as a complete overview of bear natural history, but as some historical vignettes of Yellowstone bear study. Wherever possible, I have retained the original titles used by the authors, especially in the selections from *Yellowstone Nature Notes.*

Denning and Cub Growth

Humans have always been fascinated by the mysteries of winter denning and have been charmed by the appearance and behavior of new cubs. Yellowstone afforded naturalists some unusual opportunities to observe both denning and cub rearing. Bears found it convenient to "den" under the elevated floors of park buildings and to raise their cubs in proximity of human foods, making all these activities easy to observe. At times, naturalists even took cubs from the dens for closer examination, or even to keep and raise. It all seems a little unnatural to us now, but at the time it made perfect sense, and it was fun besides.

Again, remember that the information here is not state-of-the-art. Cub adoption, for example, has since been documented in several bear populations.

1930

Adoption Among Bears
E. E. Ogston, Assistant Chief Ranger

Early May brought a black bear to the back door of Lake Ranger Station. She was a mature animal of about five years of winter hibernation. Beside here were two very small black cubs, borne by her some time in January or February.

At this time in May there were no "Messes" at Lake and the scent of the Rangers' cooking and edibles left over from the table brought her to their back door. She was an animal of most pleasing appearance and disposition and her offspring were of the same nature. Day after day mother and cubs appeared at the station and were fed.

In June a request came for the loan of one of these cubs to be taken to Moran for the filming of the picture, "The Big Trail" by Hal G. Evarts, with the understanding that the cub should be returned to its mother at Lake Station.

After enticing the little fellow into the Ranger station, the door was closed and a blanket thrown over him. He was then placed in a box, and was soon on his way to Moran. The mother walked away with only one cub and did not appear to miss the one we had taken from her. Eight days elapsed and the cub was brought back from Moran with a chain and collar on his neck. We watched for his mother but by this time many tourists had arrived and she no doubt was being fed elsewhere.

Around the Ranger station appeared another bear with two cubs. This brown bear had one black and one brown cub. Here the little black cub we had was turned loose to prove the method of so-called "adoption" among bears. That brown mother bear took a ferocious run at the orphan black cub and would have killed it if it had not climbed to safety. This cub whined and cried, but every time it started to come down the brown mother bear would charge at the tree and lacerate the bark from the tree. When this cub did come after the brown mother bear left, it started on a crusade to find its own mother and playful sister. If you have ever watched a bird dog work you will understand that cub's actions for that is what it did and was doing for no other purpose than to find its mother. For three days and nights this little fellow worked this way and at different intervals was fed by tourists and I have been informed slept in a girl's lap one evening.

Many times this brown mother appeared in the camp ground and charged this cub who always climbed a tree and proceeded out on the end of a long limb and laid on its branches, thereby safe from harm.

Tourists became aware that it had no mother, but I informed them this was a study. Finally the original mother came to the camp ground and the orphan cub was up a tree. I recognized her immediately with her one cub. I placed bread at the foot of this tree and in an instant that mother reared to her full height and scented the tree, a few affectionate grunts and the little orphan came down.

I have never witnessed such a reunion and it is beyond me to describe such a scene. Nowhere have I ever seen such common sense, and to describe the final episode, mother fondled this cub, talked to it, and cleaned it before sitting down to let her two cubs take milk from her breasts. In doing so this one cub who had been minus his milk for some time kept a continual grunting with mother in a position like the famous bear picture in the Jack Haynes collection. Moral of this story—do bears adopt cubs, I have always said no and I still claim they do not.

1931

Bringing Up Barney
Dorr Yeager, Park Naturalist

"Say, Dorr, did you hear about the bear family over at Old Faithful," said Fred, reaching for another slice of bread.

"Bear family at this time of year?" I asked.

Yep," Fred replied, applying a liberal amount of butter. "Old Barney—you know him, the winter caretaker—found a mother and a couple of cubs hibernating under one of the buildings. He pried up a board in the floor and snoops at 'em every once in a while. Says the youngsters were born January 20—about."

"Golly," I said, "I'd like to see them." But I shook my head sadly because we were talking in the mess shack at Yellowstone Park Head-quarters and Old Faithful was fifty miles and a four-day ski trip away. So we let the matter drop and went on consuming the stewed prunes.

Fate took a hand, however, and the middle of February found two of us on skis for a trip of 150 miles around the loop road. February 20 found us at Old Faithful, and it wasn't long before I was having a look at the bear family. The mother should have been, according to all the books, in a state of coma. She was not, however, and took a wide-awake and vicious slap at the floor with her paw when we peered in at her. We had to see those cubs, nevertheless, and made a grappling hook of stout wire, hoisting the month-old babies up.

They couldn't have tipped the scales at more than three pounds and looked like a pair of black puppies. Their eyes were still closed and their coats were still soft and silky. And what a row they put up! A bear cub a month old is not dumb, anyway.

That night the idea struck me. Why not take one of the cubs in to headquarters? Little information is to be found about bears of such a tender age. Here was an opportunity to observe the growth of one without constantly finding it necessary to seek shelter from a solicitous parent. We discussed the proposition pro and con. It would be no snap to get the little fellow safely over the remaining one hundred miles of ski trail, we agreed. But the pros finally triumphed and the following day we again brought the grappling hook into play. Our "fishing trip" was successful and we hoisted eight inches of squirming, twisting, squealing fur and claws up through the hole in the floor. We promptly christened him "Barney" in honor of our host, and then turned to the serious problem of nutrition.

The solution of this problem was necessary and soon became imperative. There was no such thing as a nipple at Old Faithful. The wails of the baby demanded immediate action. Necessity mothered another invention and soon the infant was contentedly gulping down diluted and sweetened condensed milk from a nursing bottle made from the rubber of an eye-dropper and an aspirin container.

If there be doubters when I state that transporting a month-old bear on skis for one hundred miles through the heart of Yellowstone is no joke, let them attempt it. Two problems confronted us. First we must keep the little fellow well fed, and we must protect him from the zero weather. The first was solved by carrying a bottle filled with milk with us. Its capacity was limited and was not actually sufficient for his needs, but it kept off the pangs of hunger during the hours of travel. The second problem was solved by wrapping him in an old sweater and tucking him into the front pocket of my parka. Several times a day he would wriggle about until his head stuck out under the flap of the pocket. Then we had to stop and rewrap him.

It was a trip marked by the painful memories of stopping along the trail to heat milk; of arising in cold snowshoe cabins to quiet a baby bear; of listening to the piercing screams emerging from the pocket of my parka as we trudged mile after mile over the unbroken snow of Yellowstone Park. Up over the Continental Divide we went—not once but four times; down across the great white expanse of Yellowstone Lake and on through Dunraven Pass, all the way to the music of a hungry and disgruntled black bear cub. True, he now and then slept, but upon awaking he would set up such a wail that I felt sure he would arouse some of his relatives from hibernation and that they would come bounding to the rescue. After seven days and nights we reached headquarters. To my surprise Barney had actually gained on the trip in spite of the hardships which he had, by necessity, undergone.

One of his eyes had opened at Yellowstone Lake and the other at the Canyon. "He's a big bear," remarked my companion seriously. "His eyes opened fifteen miles apart." The first of these organs came into use on February 25, thirty-six days after birth.

Once housed in a warm box and given regular feedings from a lambing nipple, Barney became a firm advocate of civilization. As his eyes opened wider he became more and more interested in his surroundings. The near-sightedness, so apparent in adult bears, was evident in Barney at an early age. Even when three months old, I was convinced that he could not clearly make out objects more than ten feet away from him.

Like all babies, he had difficulty in mastering the art of walking. Someone has said that the process of walking is a series of interrupted falls. This was true with Barney, only that his falls were not interrupted. He would stand on little legs wabbling pitifully under him, teetering backward and forward until he abruptly sat down or went over head first.

Eventually he learned the trick and would walk slowly across the floor lifting his feet very high in order not to trip over them. With walking, his field of investigation was greatly enlarged. Nothing within reach in the kitchen went unexplored. The rungs of chairs held a particular fascination for him. Over and under and around he would go until we felt that he must surely choke himself on one of them. Occasionally he would get so tangled amid the cross-pieces that he was helpless and required human assistance. One of the exploring expeditions nearly ended in disaster. We heard a wail and found his head firmly wedged in the U-shaped drain tap under the sink. He

Three views of the cub "Barney," Mammoth Hot Springs, 1931. National Park Service photos.

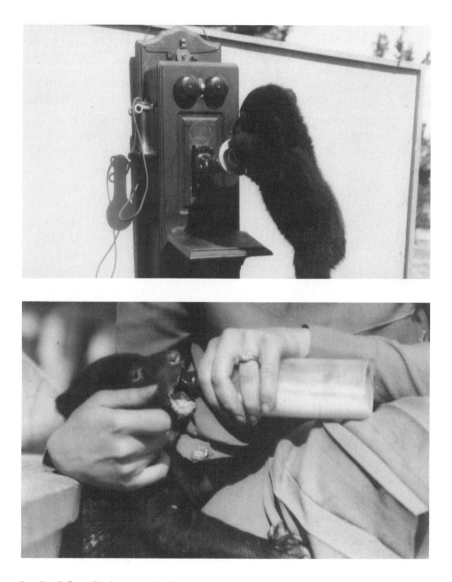

looked for all the world like a cow in a stanchion as he twisted and howled, absolutely unable to free himself. Again human aid came to the rescue of a chagrined little bear.

As time went on he learned speed and he would go scampering across the floor, under chairs and around table legs in a terrifying manner. Sometimes he would spring straight into the air and land on all fours like a young lamb. These playful moods always came on a full stomach and never seemed to possess him when his thoughts were turned to the more serious matters of eating.

Feeding Barney was a matter of great concern in the household. Certain definite precautions had to be adopted so he was never fed with the naked hands. His nurse usually wore gloves because Barney was oblivious to everything else when he was taking nourishment. His little claws pawed the air wildly and could inflict an ugly wound. At other times he evidently realized that the claws and teeth should be used with discretion, because he seemed careful not to use them when being handled. His allotment of milk was gradually increased from two ounces to four. He preferred fresh milk to the canned variety and flatly refused to take anything unless a goodly amount of sugar had been added. He consumed his food with little grunts of contentment, very human indeed, and, when finished, his stomach assumed the proportions of a small balloon. I fear that Barney became a spoiled and pampered bear.

Although not easily frightened, he did at times show fear or, perhaps better, astonishment. A sudden move on the part of a person in the room, or the presence of something new always called forth a savage little "woof" from the infant. On one occasion I happened to drop a keyring at his feet and he nearly tumbled over backward in an attempt to escape from it. His exclamation of surprise or fear in the "woof" was almost identical to that of an adult bear when disturbed.

His democratic tendencies were daily becoming more evident. He liked anyone and everyone who would play with him or rub his ears. He would crawl into their arms and caress them affectionately with his little red tongue at the first signs of friendliness on their part. These signs worried me somewhat for it seemed not unlikely that, during the coming summer, a tourist walking leisurely down the street at Headquarters would be startled when he found a cub bear loping along at his side.

It so happened that Fate took a hand in Barney's career, however. Before the tourist season opened I was transferred to Rocky Mountain National Park and we were forced to part. He went first to stay at Grand Teton National Park and is now in an eastern zoo where, reports say, he is happy, healthy and much admired.

1933

Bedroom Life of Bears
Curtis Skinner, Ranger

It is a popular belief that bears pass into a deep sleep after hibernation and continue in this somnolent state until they emerge in the spring. An old trapper once told me that he stuck a hibernating bear with a pin to see if it was alive. "It was!" he said. Even those who pass for authorities on bear life frequently refer to the "deep sleeping" of bears in winter.

At various times during the winter of 1931–'32 I had the opportunity to look in upon four different dens, in the vicinity of Old Faithful, containing adult black bear. I found none of them asleep, although they were decidedly lethargic and reluctant to move their position even when molested. Bears which I observed in their winter dens favored one characteristic position. They were always found lying belly down in a slightly dug out hole banked with twigs and grass, awake and alert. When a flashlight was played in the face of one of these semi-dormant animals, he would usually move his head from side to side, lap his jaws with his tongue, and sometimes utter deep growls. In one case, the hibernating bear could be seen clearly beneath a building without the use of a flashlight and without any disturbance from the observer. I never found him asleep. He was always alert and conscious of what was going on about him. A few daily observations recorded in the log are given below as type cases.

Feb. 15–observed brown adult bear beneath Haynes store; dopy, lethargic; would move head from side to side and lap lips with tongue; moved distance of 15 feet after being repeatedly disturbed.

Feb. 16–observed brown adult bear beneath Haynes store; restless but immovable.

Feb. 23–mother black bear beneath Haynes store uttered few deep grunts and growls when cubs were snared from nest. Also observed lone adult brown bear beneath Haynes store; lying belly down in slightly dug out hole, back arched, awake, alert.

Feb. 26–black mother bear moved cubs 30 feet.

Mar. 3–located large brown bear beneath lodge kitchen floor; growled and charged when flashlight was thrown on him. (This bear has a summer reputation of being "cross.")

Mar. 17–mother black bear and lone adult brown engaged in several noisy combats beneath Haynes store during observation. Also observed adult brown bear seen beneath hotel girls' dormitory; lethargic, moved head from side to side.

Mar. 20–crawled under hotel girls' dormitory and observed adult brown bear in den; appeared shy and timid; moved beneath building when closely approached; appeared in good condition.

Several facts lead to the conclusion that bears experience no intestinal activity during hibernation. For two weeks preceding retirement in the late fall they seem chiefly engaged in clearing the intestinal tract. During this period they eat a considerable amount of grass and roots and have very little appetite for meat and other heavy foods taken ravenously in the summer months. Body excrements become conspicuous about the exterior of their selected winter den; but no trace is found in close proximity to the den itself. Of five dens observed throughout the winter, no excrement was found in them.

That bears in their winter status have no appetite for foods, is to be concluded from a number of experiments. Towards spring, however, they will eat a small amount of food if available. These facts will best be brought out by again referring to the log.

Feb. 23–placed chicken bones, fruitcake, and honey near bear den beneath Haynes store.

Feb. 24–food not taken beneath Haynes store.

Observations made on Feb. 26, 27, 29, Mar. 3 showed that food had not been touched.

Mar. 13—food eaten.

Mar. 21—placed pineapple preserves and apple butter near same den.

Mar. 22—pineapple preserves and apple butter eaten by bears in this den.

The above observations also reveal that food was not taken immediately after being placed near den.

Emergence. The first bear around Old Faithful to emerge from his winter home was an adult black animal which was seen near the hotel girls' dormitory on the evening of March 12. An adult brown bear left his den beneath the lodge kitchen on the night of March 17; coming out regularly every night thereafter. On the night of March 17 he dug several holes in the snow near the lodge and extricated a number of empty cans, including two tobacco tins. He also found an old beef bone and divested it of flesh and gristle. Thereafter he came regularly to the garbage dump near the ranger station, and on the night of March 21 carried a burlap sack containing two dead chickens from the garbage pile to his den at the lodge, a distance of 400 yards through the snow. Dumping the chickens out of the sack at the entrance to his winter home, he retired beneath the building with his dinner of fowl.

Two adult bears, wintering beneath the cafeteria, came out for the first time on the night of March 21. Upon first emerging, they rubbed and rolled extensively in the snow about the building; then prowled about for several hours digging here and there in the snow and seeking buried garbage piles. In following their trail, I observed that they stopped frequently to roll in the snow or to rub themselves against trees or snowbanks. The snow depth around the buildings at that time was forty inches, but it was crusted sufficiently to enable them to ramble about without sinking more than twelve to eighteen inches.

Temperature moderations over short periods of time apparently have little effect in inducing bears to emerge from hibernation; although it is likely that a prolonged warm mid-winter period might bring them outside for a few days. This conclusion is drawn from the fact that during the rather warm period from February 24 to March 4 (moderate weather with temperatures 12 to 30 degrees above zero during the nights; daytime temperatures as high as 54, and extensive thawing) no bears appeared. While the first animals seen came out in temperatures ranging from 10 to 38 degrees below zero at night, accompanied by cool to cold days.

1933

More Denning Bears
John F. Alton, Ranger

Two bears were under observation at Old Faithful during the winter of 1932–'33. These bears will be referred to in the following as Nos. 1 & 2.

The bears spent the latter part of October preparing their winter nests. The nests were very similar and were made of twigs, chips, small stones, grasses (roots and tops), pine cones, pine needles, rags, paper, and pine bark. A hollow was scooped out of the earth by the bear. The nest was made in this hollow with the sides built up about ten inches above the center. In each case the long way of the nest extended north and south.

After the nest was prepared the bears spent most of the days in the open abstaining from food and clearing their alimentary canal. They appeared drowsy and exerted themselves very little during the period between the completion of their nests and the actual retiring to them for the winter.

The last time they were seen out was on November 28.

Bear #1 lent itself to ready observation as its nest was only some ten feet from a trap-door in the floor of the Old Faithful Lodge. The bear was a large mature, male, black bear, brown in color.

Bear #2 spent the winter under the Old Faithful Cafeteria. Observations were easily made until the first shoveling of snow became necessary shortly after the first of January. After the first removal of snow from the building some 6 to 12 feet of snow blocked the entrance to the nest for the remainder of the winter. The bear was a large mature, male, black bear, black in color.

Each bear was in practically total darkness all winter. The nests were built on cold ground. Snow piled high around three sides of bear #1 and some snow remained on the remaining side during the entire winter. Snow piled high all around the nest of bear #2. The thermometer went down to –60°F. at one time during the winter.

The following observations were made during the winter:

Bear #1

Date	Direction Headed	Awake or Asleep	Hour of Observation
12-2-32	south	drowsy	2:00 P.M.
12-11-32	south	more drowsy	10:00 A.M.
12-29-32	south	very drowsy	8:00 P.M.
1-6-33	south	a little wider awake	10:00 A.M.
1-22-33	north	drowsy	7:00 P.M.
1-29-33	south	very much awake	3:00 P.M.
2-9-33	north	very much awake	9:00 A.M.
2-18-33	south	awake	9:00 A.M.
2-27-33	south	awake	11:00 P.M.
3-1-33	north	awake	3:00 P.M.
3-6-33	south	awake	2:30 P.M.
3-7-33	south	awake	7:00 A.M.
3-15-33	south	wide awake	9:00 A.M.
3-25-33	Bear came out of nest during the night until May 13 when he started coming out during the day		

Bear #2

Date	Direction Headed	Awake or Asleep	Hour of Observation
12-2-32	south	awake	1:30 P.M.
12-11-32	south	drowsy	9:00 A.M.
12-29-32	north	very drowsy	3:00 P.M.
1-6-33	south	not so drowsy	10:15 A.M.
1-22-33	south	awake	1:00 P.M.

Candy was placed by the nest of bear #1 at 2:30 P.M. on March 6. He was not observed eating this candy, however, it disappeared before 7:00 A.M. on March 7. It is probable that some other animal may have eaten it.

Summary: 1. The bears were conscious at all times, during observations, of any activity going on about them.

2. The conditions mentioned above offer a fair comparison to the conditions under which other bears pass the winter in this section of the country.

1933

A Grizzly Den
Herbert Lystrup, Ranger Naturalist

On July 20 of this year District Ranger Childs, Ranger Dougherty, and I hiked to the top of the Madison Plateau, south of the Black Sand Basin to determine the feasibility of a temporary fire look-out station. While there we took occasion to visit a rock cave known to be a hibernating den of grizzlies in the winter.

After a difficult climb we came upon an old trail which we followed for a short distance, then left it, working our way out through the timber and rocks to the edge of the cliff. Here the rock was rhyolite and its well altered condition indicated that it had once been acted upon by hot waters. Under one of the huge blocks we saw above us the approach to a large cave. The trail leading up to the entrance was well worn and tracks were so distinct that there seemed to be an excellent possibility that the cave might even now be inhabited.

The outer chamber or entrance was about 20 feet by 20 feet by 10 feet high. Before entering we shouted lustily and tossed in some rocks, but there was no response. So we scrambled up the incline to the smaller opening and began our explorations in earnest. The smaller opening was located some fifteen feet beyond the main entrance and was about three feet in diameter. We crawled into this to find a very comfortable den about three feet high and nine feet in diameter. To my surprise there were no bad odors and no evidence of bear excreta. The place was neat and orderly and the floor bare and smooth. In the center was a hollowed out nest-like structure lined with bits of sticks, grass, withered moss, pine and spruce cones, and some horse dung. We concluded that this nest, about eighteen inches in diameter, was the bed in which the little cubs had snuggly slept during the long cold winter nights. The den seemed an ideal place protected from wintry blasts, especially since the outer cave would likely become well filled with drifting snow, and shut out the winds. Such is the comfortable home in which the American grizzly leisurely sleeps through the long severe winters so common to the Yellowstone.

1938

Hibernation of Bears
William E. Kearns, Assistant Naturalist

Not long ago, I read an article in the Saturday Evening Post by J. Frank Dobie on "The Last of the Grizzly Hunters." The statement that bears "lay up and suck their paws," (hibernate) from "November for four months," caused me to do a bit of investigating of the "theories" for bears hibernating.

Here in Yellowstone, the beginning is largely determined by the weather, but the majority of both grizzly and black bears go into hibernation in October and November. The earlier the snows come and the colder the weather, the sooner the bear seeks out his den. When seasonal conditions are more favorable, some of the bears may remain out as late as December. The period spent in hibernation will vary from four to five months, and here again, weather plays an important role, and is often the deciding factor. A few bears may appear in February, but it is usually mid-March or even the first of April before the majority appear.

Few actual observations have been made of wild bears in hibernation, and in the time of my father and other old timers, supposition and conjecture took the place of fact. With some, the belief was rampant that all bears gorged themselves on pine needles immediately before going into their dens for the "all-winter sleep," assuming that these needles would form a lining in the bear's stomach and keep him from getting hungry before the weather moderated and he could again find food. Still another, as suggested by Mr. Dobie, was that the animal would suck his paws, until by spring they were too sore for the bear to more than hobble about.

With the majority, the belief is still current that an animal in hibernation loses all consciousness, and that bodily processes slow down to a point where the heart scarcely beats and the blood barely flows. With the Marmot and the Picket Pin this is true, but not so for either the grizzly or black bear found in Yellowstone. Observations made in specially constructed dens indicate that the bear is not absolutely in a state of coma, but rather, the opposite. Upon the approach of the observer, the bear would move, sometimes growl, and open-eyed, would repel the annoyer if too aggravated. While on a ski trip around the grand loop during the winter of 1935, I went to visit the den of a black bear in the hope of getting pictures. His winter quarters were beneath the floor of the kitchen of the lodge at Old Faithful and near a trap door. Lifting this door, I lowered my camera and the necessary paraphernalia to the ground some four feet beneath, intending to follow. Fortunately, I looked first with the aid of a flashlight and saw a large black bear moving toward me as rapidly as the floor joists would permit. Hastily retrieving my outfit, I just had time to lower the door, closing it almost in the bear's face.

Usually the bears select some spot not so accessible for man, and authentic pictures of bears in hibernation are rare. Dens beneath buildings are often used, natural caves, wind-falls in dense timber offer quarters, and the big animals often dig their own den. Strange as it may seem, the site is usually on the north slope of a hill. It would seem reasonable that a den dug in the warmer south slope, which is freed from snow at an earlier date, would be the preference, but not so with bruin. Here again, the bear is wise for the prevailing winds are from the southwest and the snow piles deeply on the north slopes, covering the dens with a thick, warm blanket which helps to keep out the bitter cold of winter.

On January 1, 1937, Junior Naturalist Oberhansley led a party of fifteen people on a ski trip to visit the den of a black bear which was hibernating on the northern slope of a hill to the north of Mammoth. Although the party proceeded as quietly as possible on nearing the den, the bear was wide awake and came to within 4½ feet of the entrance. The opening of this den was about 1½ feet across, and had been dug into the hillside in the midst of a small stand of cedar trees. This bear came out of hibernation on March 7. He did not eat the heavily crusted snow, contrary to other observations when bears had eaten quantities of the icy substance, and after basking in the sun for a short time, this bear retired to his den for another nap.

This last summer, road crews at Fishing Bridge constructed a heavily oiled surfaced road in front of the operator's buildings. Beneath the Haynes Picture Shop was a den which a black bear had used for several winters. When Mr. Bear returned late in October to look over his winter apartment, he found the entrance entirely blocked with a thick section of roadway. Undaunted, he tore away the hard, almost rock-like surface in huge chunks, and proceeded with preparations of his winter bed.

Mrs. Pierson called me on the phone the other day to tell me that while her husband, Dave Pierson, with Tom Phillips and Rudy Schmidt, were out feeding hay to the buffalo at the Buffalo Ranch on January 22, they observed a small black bear, probably a two year old, come from the direction of Druid Peak and disappear up the slopes of Specimen Ridge. He was very thin, and one of the boys suggested that he might be sick.

The next morning, the feeders frightened him from the haystack where he had dug-in and the bear ran toward a distant stack. He was not observed eating hay. Monday morning about 9:30 A.M., the little fellow was again seen, headed for a near by stack. From all appearances, the coyotes had pre-empted his bed of the night before. The bear was seen almost daily and his condition was so pitiful that the men fed him scraps nearly every morning. A week after he was first observed, he spent the night sleeping on top of the hay and although the thermometer registered 37 degrees below zero, he was up and ready for breakfast Sunday morning. As suddenly as he had appeared, the bear vanished, probably in a newly acquired den in one of the numerous haystacks.

Several days later, the Piersons reported that a second two-year old black bear was in the vicinity, and that he had moved in to dine on the contents of the garbage cans at the Ranch House. This second bear was in much better condition than number one, and was marked quite differently so that there was no doubt as to his identity. Mrs. Pierson stated that "he seems to hear alright, but from the half-baked way in which he acts, his eyesight must not be right." When a person approached, the bear would jump, raise his head, and finally seem to smell-out the source of the disturbance. It has been suggested that he may have been suffering form snow-blindness.

The second arrival wasn't satisfied with the scanty fare afforded at the garbage cans, and moved in on the Piersons' porch where he helped himself to bacon and butter, and later made-up his bed on their back porch. The latest report (February 14) is that this bear is still at the Ranch and eating from the garbage cans.

Wondering how many instances of this sort had been recorded, I perused back issues of *Nature Notes* with the following results: in the issue of February 28, 1926, this item concerning bears is noted:

"On the 6th of January, a large black bear and three cubs were outside at the rear of the Lake Hotel. The old bear is seen nearly every day. In coming out they are very careful to keep in the same tracks on paths made on previous trips and do not exert themselves very much. These bears have taken for their winter abode the cook's quarters of the hotel. The place left open is not large and underneath the floor makes a good den for them. Even after the snow was on they spent many hours pulling coarse slough grass and dragging it in for a bed. It seems possible now that the old bear will be out almost every day during the winter, if fed."

Ranger "Ben" Arnold who was at Lake the winter of 1925–1926 as winterkeeper for the lodge, relates the incident of two big black bears, "Nicodemus and Nebuchadnezzar," coming out from their hibernation den under the hotel building after the trails were well packed, and states that they remained out more or less all winter. On one occasion, they "stole" a pair of pants belonging to Ed Admunsen, hotel winterkeeper, from the clothes line and took them to the den, supposedly for lining. (Al was a big fellow, and they were an immense pair of pants!) On another escapade they visited the laundry room of the hotel and removed a heavy fabric belt from one of the machines. Dragging it to their den, they chewed it until it was ruined for further use. These two bears visited the garbage cans of the rangers and winterkeepers, but did not venture from the beaten trails at any time.

A further reference in *Nature Notes* is found in the issue of February 28, 1927, as follows:

"A large black bear that has been hibernating under the hotel at Yellowstone Lake appeared on the trails in the vicinity of the buildings on the 19th of February. He was out during an interval of two days. His activities consisted in part, of the theft of a ham from the winterkeeper and after finding nothing further of interest he returned to his den. This is the first and only activity of bears reported since late last fall, with the exception of the captive bear, Juno, at headquarters station. Frequent visits have been made to his den during the past two months and we find that he is easily aroused but is very sluggish in his movements. He accepts very little food and rarely emerges from the den. His disposition is harmless and gentle."

Mrs. Marguerite L. Arnold informs me that several years ago, former Park Naturalist Edmund Sawyer attempted to feed Juno, the chained pet, while he was in hibernation, but she states, "the bear just wasn't interested."

On Christmas day, Ranger David Condon saw a black bear running across the firing-line just north of the Park, and on January 8, Junior Naturalist F. R. Oberhansley viewed the carcass of a bear in the same vicinity. These men surmise that this animal might have been literally bombarded out of his den by the heavy firing of the hunters massed in the area, and that the bear was unable to make good his escape.

Bears have been observed outside their dens in winter at various times through the years, usually after unseasonably warm days, but with the exceptions noted (with others unrecorded and unknown), the bears did not go more than a step or two from the entrance of their dens.

From actual observations of bears in hibernation, we know then, that they sleep for indefinite periods, are restless at times, even to leaving their dens, and that when on such foraging expeditions they may eat. However, as far as I've been able to ascertain, the bear in hibernation will not eat. Ranger Frank Childs offered bacon and sweets to several bears while they were hibernating, but without exception, they refused the proffered food.

1948

Canyon Bear Apartments
Wayne Replogle, Park Ranger Naturalist

The possibilities of studying bear dens in the Canyon area is unlimited and some important facts concerning these are being presented.

The most outstanding hibernation area that I have found yet is a group of four separate dens in the rim rock area just southwest of the Canyon Auto Camp.

Going through the camp one reaches at the far side an old wooden bridge over which the road goes to reach the camping area above Pryor's store. To reach the apartment house one stops at the bridge and follows the trail to the left up a shallow ravine slightly north-westward for 250 feet until he arrives at the two large hollowed rocks. To the left and up the grassy slope about 50 feet is the rim rock under which will be found the four "apartments." Counting from left to right we will number them 1, 2, 3 and 4.

No. 1 is an open den some thirty feet long in which two or three bears could easily "hole up." The face of the den is protected by drifting snow.

No. 2 is an individual den, excellently proportioned for one bear or a mother and cubs. It will be found about forty feet to the right of Den No. 1 and at the same level.

No. 3 is the most remarkable den I have ever found. The opening is broad with an excellent vestibule. Inside, a hallway reaches for ten or fifteen feet which is eight feet wide and four feet high. At the far end of the hallway the den opens into a room about twenty feet long, twelve feet wide and six feet high, cut out of obsidian sand, and breccia. These materials are decomposing very rapidly leaving the floor several feet deep with sand. The boulders, which were imbedded in the breccia, have been removed for the most part. The inner room shows some dampness but not excessively so. In the main room are two large beds and two small beds. The remarkable thing is the fact that it shows that more than one adult bear will hibernate in the same den along with possibly one or two younger bears.

No. 4 is also an excellent example of a choice of a winter home. Through a long tube-like hallway, sloping upward, some twenty feet long, large enough only for a single bear to pass at a time, there leads to a perfect bed about five feet by five feet by five feet. In this bed on August 17, 1948, I found a large supply of recently pulled grass, most of it green, strewn over the bed. I would guess that due to its freshness it wasn't more than a day old. Some tufts of hair were found caught on the jagged edges of the ceiling rocks at the doorway.

Small finger sized sticks were found in all the beds. This remarkable colony of dens is accessible to the public and if past interest in bear dens is an indication I'm sure large numbers of our guests will be anxious to visit the dens in the future.

Food Habits

Even at the height of the dump-feeding days, bears did not abandon other food sources. Behavior that is now being documented in great depth, such as grizzly predation on elk calves and spawning trout, was observed long ago. The great variety of bear foods was revealed by some studies, though even today researchers are still discovering previously undocumented food choices among bears.

Perhaps the biggest surprise in the following accounts may be how adept park bears are at capturing large mammals. Though it is true that bears may spend most of their time grazing or digging for plant foods, they also have exceptional skills as hunters. Notice, however, that in the accounts by Way and Abbie the bears do not always have their way with the prey in question: predators are no more assured of survival than are the animals they pursue.

1921

A Hunting Black Bear
A. Brazier Howell

On June 12, 1920, while approaching a camping site on the Lamar River, Yellowstone National Park, in company with M. P. Skinner, park naturalist, I noted a black bear hunting around through the sage brush on a nearby hillside. Five minutes later we stopped for the night, and as I descended from the machine, I turned my ten power glasses on the bear, and was surprised to see that he was making off, at a leisurely gait, with an elk calf in his mouth. He paid not the slightest attention to the presumable mother of the calf, which followed him anxiously within fifteen or twenty feet; she, in turn, being followed by three other cows. Shortly, the bear entered a small grove of aspens into which the cows were afraid to follow, and they walked back and forth along the border of this for some time. Three of the cows soon dispersed, but the fourth wandered about disconsolately until dark.

When with the cows, the elk calves are reasonably safe, but the latter are usually hidden in the brush or forest while their mothers are feeding in the meadows, and it is at such times that the bears have a chance to make a meal, which opportunity, according to Skinner, they never fail to embrace. I have observed the "hidden" calves in the woods, and have noticed that as long as a person is in motion, although only six feet away, the calves remain absolutely still, with neck extended along the ground, but the instant the person stops, they are up and sprawling through the timber at their best gait. These notes may be of interest to those who contend that the black bear is harmless to game, and confines his attentions to more humble fare.

1930

Cannibal Bear
Ben Arnold, Park Ranger

The bear question in Yellowstone Park recently developed another angle. We now have big ones eating little ones. Our friendly clowns, the bears, have been called a lot of hard names by tourists unfamiliar with their habits. The word cannibal may be a welcome addition to overworked vocabularies. This particular case involves "Brownie" or brown bear, mother of five month old twin cubs, who did maliciously pursue, attack and kill a five month old black cub, being one of "Rosie's" spring twins.

Rosie is a black bear and all summer has been Brownie's partner in crime, with headquarters at the bear cafeteria near Roosevelt Camp. The two mothers with their twin babies have afforded endless amusement to Tower Falls tourists this season and thousands of photographs have been taken of them.

Early one morning Brownie was seen in hot pursuit of the black cub, chasing it over a nearby hill. The pitiful cries of the little fellow first attracted attention. For some reason he failed to "tree" and before help could reach him had been killed and terribly mangled. The carcass was left there after chasing Brownie away. Further investigation that evening found Brownie and her cubs with the carcass. It had been carried 200 yards under a large fir tree; one cub was up the tree; the others cleaning up last vestiges of skeleton and hide.

1933

Some Bears Get Their Share of Fish

J. Thomas Stewart, Jr., Ranger-Naturalist

It is estimated that about eighty thousand cutthroat, or native trout, are taken from the waters fo Yellowstone Lake and River every season by man. This trout was native to these waters when man first came to the park and today it is the only fish found in Yellowstone Lake in any quantity. The U.S. Bureau of Fisheries works constantly to insure a supply of cutthroat trout for this wonderful fishing area for it is certain that under the natural propagation alone the waters would be depleted. However, the men employed in this work of trapping the female fish and taking their eggs to be hatched in the hatchery have their troubles with the bears.

Bears are great consumers of fish when they can get them and the traps built by the hatchery men are often visited by hungry bears. On June 30 of last season the chief ranger and the writer found a bear enjoying a fine feast of fish from a trap in Bridge Bay. If there is a sufficient supply at hand the bear does not eat the heads of the fish but piles them neatly to one side. On occasion fifty-two heads were found left by a bear after one meal.

Many methods have been tried to keep the bears from robbing the fish traps. One plan adopted was to drive long spikes through the trap to greet the sensitive nose of the snooping bear but Bruin quickly discovered that no spikes had been driven through the bottom of the traps so with his powerful forepaws he turned the trap over and entered from the other side, eating what he wanted and allowing the rest to escape. Another method in which man has matched his wits against the cleverness of a bear is to place some spark coils and batteries in such a manner as to connect them up with wires on the traps. For a time this seemed to keep the bears away but finally one, more persistent than the rest, discovered that the pain inflicted by the large batteries lasted for only a few minutes and that if this were endured he could obtain a delectable meal in a very short time. It seems that this was discovered by other bears for it was not long until a large number were visiting the electrified traps. And so it seems that the ingenuity of man is often matched by the cleverness of the bears for they are persistent and will return again and again to a point where food is available and the problems of the hatchery people to keep the streams and lakes of Yellowstone Park supplied with trout are always changing.

1937

Some Food Habits of the Black Bear

Adolph Murie

In the Jackson Hole–Yellowstone region, during the summer of 1935, grasshoppers and crickets were more abundant than usual. Autoists on the Cooke City highway leading out of Yellowstone reported that in the higher areas the dead bodies of crickets made the road almost slippery. Grasshoppers and crickets are hard on vegetation, but the bears revelled in the insects, particularly the crickets, for these were the more abundant where the bears were active. The bears were observed feeding on these insects on August 23 on the high grassy ridges between Cache Creek and Miller Creek, and on the slopes north of Cache Creek, in the upper Lamar River region in Yellowstone Park.

The first day out we had to hurry to reach our destination so there was but little time for making observations. Also, for much of the time we followed streams, which apparently were not then frequented by the bears. We saw only a single bear and had but a glimpse of it as it entered a patch of timber. The second day we travelled in the timber up Miller Creek and saw neither bears nor bear sign.

We spent the third day wandering over the open park-like ridges examining the bison range. The hillsides were flecked with bison chips of all ages and I was astonished to see that hundreds of these had been tipped over by the bears. I tipped over several myself to see what they harbored, and found a cricket or two or a grasshopper under some of them. Only chips that had reached a certain age were potential hiding places for crickets, as the younger chips adhered too closely to the ground to afford any shelter.

During the day we saw 11 bears—6 adults and 5 cubs. At noon we saw the first, a mother and two cubs on a far hill-side feeding on the ground. About an hour later we approached the spot and found the adult still foraging. She slowly moved her nose over the ground, picking up a cricket every step or two and giving each one a few bites before swallowing it. There was no difficulty in catching the crickets, for the coolness of the day made them very inactive and sluggish. Most of the crickets were picked up in the grass, but some were taken under bison chips. With a paw the chip was delicately tipped on one edge and held poised while she peered beneath to see what was uncovered. The chips were probably turned over from force of habit gained in areas where such routine procedure was required to find food, for here the chips yielded but little compared to the number that could be picked up in the open. We approached within 50 yards of the bear before she discovered us. She emitted a hoarse snort that sent her two cubs scampering in unison, one on each side of the trunk, to the very top of a spruce. The mother continued to go through the motions of feeding until she had gained the edge of a grove, where she sat watching us.

On another hillside was an adult with a cub, and separated from them by several hundred yards was another lone adult. These bears were likewise searching over the open slopes for crickets and grasshoppers.

North of Cache Creek we frightened a lone bear at the edge of a grove and nearby found a fresh dropping composed of crickets and grasshoppers, which indicated that this bear also had been feeding on these insects. About one-half mile away there was still another lone bear, and a short distance beyond was a mother with two cubs. In the neighborhood of these four bears were a number of fresh bear droppings composed entirely of crickets and grasshoppers.

Scattered over the hillsides where the bears had been feeding lay many bear droppings. Most of them were relatively fresh, presumably not over two weeks old. Three droppings formed of grass were old and it is likely that they represented food eaten before the crickets became available. A total of 64 droppings were examined with the following results: 58 of them were composed entirely of crickets and grasshoppers, mainly the former; 3 contained crickets and grasshoppers with a small admixture of some berry, probably huckleberry; and 3 contained grass. The hard parts of the insects, such as the legs, ovipositor, and the head, were often entire, rendering identification very easy.

Apparently the bears in the hills at this time were living entirely on crickets and grasshoppers. It was thought by some that the bears had deserted the park garbage piles for the purpose of gorging themselves on these entomological sweets. If this were true then the crickets and the grasshoppers must be given due credit for attracting the bears to the hills, for encouraging them to desert the garbage pile to live a clean out-of-doors life where bears are bears.

1942

Grizzly and Bull Elk Battle
Lester Abbie

On May 20th as I drove the snow plow around a bend of the road between Lava Creek and Blacktail Deer Creek I saw a large bull elk near the road with what appeared to be a man leading him. As I approached nearer the apparent man proved to be a medium sized Grizzly bear which was reared up on his hind legs endeavoring to kill the elk.

This large bull had shed his antlers and the new growth was very small, so he had entered this struggle handicapped by the absence of his most useful weapon, the long sharp tines of the mature antlers.

The two combatants were fighting at close quarters, the elk fighting for his life, the bear endeavoring to kill, probably for food. The bear had the elk gripped around the neck with his forepaws and was endeavoring to throw the elk, after the fashion of a rodeo performer bulldogging a steer. The elk in turn was endeavoring to get free and by so doing was shoving the bear around backward along the road. Thus from my vantage point I had thought that the elk was being led by someone.

I stopped the snowplow and taking my camera started out to try and photograph the incident. This action on my part disrupted the battle temporarily, for the elk broke loose from the bear and started running away. He seemed partially stunned from his encounter. The bear ran right beside him and kept reaching out his paw now and then to slap the elk on the side of the head. The elk by this time appeared to be about exhausted for his tongue was lolling out and he seemed wobbly.

The slapping action of the bear soon caused the elk to stop and fight again, this time charging the bear, which reared to his hind legs again. The bull's head struck the grizzly in the stomach and the bear then grabbed the elk around the neck. With all of his strength the elk would bunt the bear, each time raising the bear's hind feet from the ground. Shortly the elk became so tired that the bear's weight brought him to his knees.

While all of this was happening I had approached quite near the animals and suddenly the Grizzly sensed my presence. He reared up, sniffed, snorted, and allowed the elk to get up and stagger off into the woods. The Grizzly became frightened and ran away apparently suffering none from the elk's efforts to protect itself.

On my return trip I saw no further evidence of either the mature bull elk nor the Grizzly bear which I had guessed as being about four years old. Whether the bear finally succeeded in relocating his prey has remained a question in my mind.

1942

Grizzly Bears Get Food
Thomas Thompson

On May 29, 1942 at about 4 o'clock in the afternoon while I was putting up signs along the highway near the Gibbon Meadows I witnessed a wildlife incident seldom seen by human beings.

When I stopped I noted a small herd of elk, about a dozen or so, on the right bank of the Gibbon River about 300 yards away, and across the River from me. The herd appeared to consist of cows, a few of which were lying down. Suddenly they got up and all of the elk started to run. After running a short ways they stopped and looked back up the river. I, too, looked up the river to see what had startled them and I saw close to the bank a Grizzly mother with three yearling cubs coming down stream toward the spot that the elk just left. A light snow was falling and visibility was not real good, but I could tell by her determined gait and the hump on her shoulder that she was a Grizzly.

When the Grizzly and bear cubs came to the spot where the elk had been lying down they commenced to beat the bush, and search for something. She and the cubs spread out, searching on the ground first to the right and then to the left making short jumps as they searched for their prey. After a few jumps I heard a squeal and I knew that they had scared up a calf elk. On investigation and closer observation I found that they had two calves instead of the one. The mother Grizzly was after one and the cubs were after the other. They would get the calves down and then the calves would bob up again, and try to get away.

The squealing of the calves brought back four or five cows close to the bears in an effort to protect their young and I started to blow the horn of my automobile. The cubs stood up and looked all around for a second and then started to run away so I kept blowing the horn. Then the mother grizzly started to run back up the river in the direction the cubs had gone. She ran about a hundred and fifty feet, stopped, turned around, and came back to pick up the calf elk she had dropped. She got the calf and went back up the river. She carried it about a quarter of a mile, dropping it several times, and finally went on out of sight into the timber where the cubs had disappeared. I kept blowing the horn all this time and probably saved the life of the calf elk which the cubs had been after. With the bears' disappearance into the woods the interesting experience came to an end.

Grizzly Bear
in Pelican Meadows

Earl M. Semingsen, District Park Ranger

In mid-October 1946 Ranger Nyquist and I were packing winter rations and supplies to the Pelican Creek patrol cabin. We were traveling about mid-way between the Pelican Creek fire road bridge and the cabin, when, as we rounded a point of timber in the meadows, our attention was centered on a large Grizzly Bear out in the sage brush and grasses. At first glance the animal appeared to be a large dark colored tree stump. We were about 100 yards away when it heard us talking or the noises from the horses' hoofs aroused its interest. The bear first reared full length and stood on its hind feet to take a quick look at us, then quickly turned and ran about 10 yards in the opposite direction from us. It then just as quickly turned and came in our direction on a dead run. For a brief moment I thought it may have decided to stand its ground or charge our small pack outfit. However, it returned to the same spot in the meadow where we first observed it. Then was when we realized that the bear was feasting on some animal that had been killed. When the grizzly arrived at the kill he made several hurried attempts to snatch an extra bite.

By that time our yelling and war-whoop sounds apparently fright-ened him for he turned away, running full speed toward the timber which was about 200 yards distance. When the bear reached the timber he took another upright look at us, then ran into the woods. Bill Nyquist and I continued down the trail with our horses for they were heavily packed and we had quite a journey ahead. Looking in the direction that the bear had run from us, we saw two grizzlies standing upright and nervously looking us over. These animals were about 500 yards from the trail.

After arriving at the cabin we unpacked our horses, stored the supplies in the cellar and otherwise attended to work necessary to prepare the place for winter. I stepped out the cabin door to check on the horses for it was snowing heavily; visibility was estimated at 300 yards distance. Glancing over the small meadow by the creek that flows near the cabin I thought I noticed a movement in the sage brush and on closer observation I was sure a large clump of snow-covered sage brush was taking off slowly to apparently transplant itself. Then I called to Bill who was munching a graham cracker and peanut butter sandwich (Nyquist's favorite—you should hear him give the Nor-wegian dialect and facial expressions on this delicacy). When Bill came to the door we watched a snow-covered grizzly root and grub out morsels of food. The animal could not hear us talking low during the howling wind and snow storm. After watching him patiently scratch about for his meal, Bill asked, "Shall we give him the works?" meaning our usual yelling, war hooping, and jumping around like a couple of wild Indians. It was agreeable with me so we let him have the first blast of scary sounds. At first the bear apparently could not accurately detect the direction from which these crazy noises were coming; however he acted quite normal and stood on his hind feet looking in a 180-degree arc for something. When we gave him our second blast of yells with motions indescribable, the bear located us and immediately reversed and ran into the timber taking one more good look at us before leaving our sight.

On our return from the cabin to the Lake Ranger Station that day, we planned our approach to the meadow where we observed the grizzly feasting on a kill, so that we might see more bear then previously. As we rode up over the top of a rolling knoll, we were surprised to see only one grizzly feasting on the kill; however there were two (mother and a cub) about 700 yards from the scene that had apparently been eating there and had moved away in deference to the huge male that was on the feasting grounds. Two others were at the edge of the timber nearest the kill. Since the feasting bear did not see or hear us we decided to see how close we could approach to the animal before he would. We continued on toward him at a normal horse walk and rode within 50 yards of the animal in the open meadow before he noticed our presence. Like the others he wheeled and ran very swiftly to the timber, not stopping for a second look as we had expected him to. Upon observation and examination of the scene of the kill, it was learned that a mature buffalo had been the big attraction for the grizzlies observed there. The buffalo was practically 100% consumed, only a small piece of hide, a few skull bones, and the feet remaining, together with the paunch and a large quantity of scattered undigested food. The sage brush and grasses immediately around the kill were trampled down over an area about 30 feet in diameter.

During this eventful day seven Grizzly Bear had been seen by us in Pelican meadows under the spell of the primitive. The day's events will remain as a memory of Yellowstone's never-ending possibilities to offer to everyone the wilderness unadulterated in all its pristine glory. No doubt there are many bear that live in this area since food for them is plentiful. One hundred and twenty six buffalo were counted in the meadows the following day together with numerous herds of elk.

1950

The Law of the Wild
Harvey B. Reynolds, Park Ranger

Mother Nature is popularly characterized as a lovable and benevolent old lady who is very busy mothering and caring for her vast numbers of birds, animals, insects and plants. Nature in fact is often of much grimmer aspect. Her harsh character is most evident in the spring when the young of various kinds are unable to defend themselves against the various predators.

For those of us who live in the Lamar Valley this is especially evident when the elk are calving. Almost daily during this season we came upon a mother elk with a newborn calf which was besieged by anywhere from two to seven coyotes. Evidently one coyote alone never tries to worry a mother elk. It takes at least two to play the grim game. While the mother is busy chasing one coyote to a safer distance from her calf another coyote dashes in and snaps at the calf before the mother can return to it. With the number of coyotes increased to seven we can well imagine what chance the mother has of protecting the young calf. One ranger tells of watching seven coyotes worry a mother elk until she was too weak to chase them and could only protect the calf by standing with her body over it. The coyotes came in and killed the calf under the mother's body.

When the calves are older and able to travel they become members of a herd which is waiting in the valley until the melting snows will allow them to migrate to summer pastures in the higher mountains. Then the herd assumes some measure of responsibility for protection of its calves. When coyotes approach the calves the mature animals will surround them and by numbers alone they are able to daunt the courage of any pack of coyotes. The herd will even try to extend protection from the huge grizzly bear as I was able to observe this spring.

I had been working for sometime on the bench meadow across the river from the Lamar Ranger Station when my attention was attracted to the wild flight of a herd of some sixty head of elk from the river bottom to a piece of higher ground directly below me. Truly I had a grandstand seat from which to watch the action that followed. The herd was pursued at some distance by three mature grizzlies. Three calves in the herd were soon outdistanced by the mature elk and dropped far behind. The herd wheeled in a complete circle and picked up the calves again. This method of picking up the calves was repeated at least four times. However, each time the pursuing bears were closer to the calves and on one such circle the calves were picked up just ahead of the bears. This time one calf darted past the herd instead of running with it and was quickly downed by the three bears. I could hear the terrified bleating of the calf for some little time after the bears had downed it. No doubt they began eating without bothering to kill the calf.

1951

Survival of the Fittest
Joe J. Way, Supervisory Park Ranger

While on a patrol up the Lamar Valley on June 11, 1951 I had a new and unusual experience which is the first of this type that I have had in the many years I have spent traveling through the Yellowstone countryside. Phillip Modesitt was traveling with me and when we reached the vicinity of Chalcedony Creek we came upon the carcass of a grizzly bear which appeared to be mutilated.

It is unusual, as a matter of fact exceedingly rare, for a man in the field to come upon a carcass of this species. From all physical evidence the large female grizzly had not been dead for any great length of time. It is my estimate that she had met death within three or four days prior to my discovering her for the scavengers of the wild had not yet started to work on the carcass.

Since it is unusual to find a dead grizzly, I made a complete examination of the bear and the surrounding countryside in an attempt to determine what might have been the cause of death. From the evidence observed it seemed very certain that the bear had in all probability been killed by a buffalo.

Upon examination it was found that both sides of the grizzly bear were badly battered and bruised to a bloody mass and the left side of the animal was punctured between the ribs by a hole 1½ inches in diameter. The immediate area around the carcass was well torn up giving evidence of a severe struggle between the bear and some other beast. There were many large buffalo tracks which had cut up the ground in an arc around the carcass and there were several patches of buffalo hair. All of this helped Modesitt and me mentally visualize the terrific struggle which had undoubtedly taken place to bring about the death of this monarch of the wild. An examination of the general area did not reveal any buffalo carcass nor an injured animal.

We left the area with a pronounced respect for the power and might which a huge bison must have in order to conquer, kill and so badly mutilate a grizzly.

1954

A Case of Bear Cannibalism
Thomas F. Ela, District Park Ranger

On October 17, 1953, in the evening, it was reported to the Ranger's station at Old Faithful, that there was a black bear cub lying dead in the road three miles east of Old Faithful. According to the reporting visitor, the sow and one other cub were keeping guard and were thus in danger of being struck by a car after dark. This had been the fate of the victim cub seen lying in a small pool of blood which was oozing from its mouth. I went to the scene of the accident but could not find the animal.

On the following morning, I returned to the scene and found the bloodstains in the road and also discovered the sow and live cut about 50 yards north of the highway. The bloodstains left off to drag marks and bear tracks on the road shoulder and adjacent damp swampy ground and then the dead cub was found lying about fifteen yards east of the sow and partially hidden. With great difficulty the sow and live cub were driven away and I brought the dead cub to the pick-up truck. There, examination showed the animal to have an unbroken body but the head was missing and so was the right hind leg although the skin was still nearly whole in each case. The ears and forehead skin was completely undamaged but lower jaw, nose and skull and all muscles were missing back to the first vertebra of the neck. The femur of the right leg was completely stripped of all muscle and stood exposed in the roll of leg skin. The foot and lower leg bones were completely missing. The skin was licked clean in each case.

Diligent search then revealed several piles of Vaccinium, grass, and small forest litter about 18 inches to two feet wide and ten inches high which smelled very strongly of bear. Each pile was then torn apart and two small pieces of cranium were found; the upper palate complete with teeth and nasal sinuses, and the almost complete lower jaw in two pieces. All flesh was stripped away from the bones and the ends of bones were chewed away and everything licked clean before the bones were hidden in the piles of vegetation. Fresh bear feces were found under similar heaps of material but there was absolutely no evidence of other animals at the scene.

A large black bear boar was seen about 300 yards up the road and another sow, with two small cubs in a nearby tree, was stationed about 100 yards away in the forest. Thus, it is obvious that the cannibalism was due to one or more of the bears present and more probably by one of the three mature bears. Since the mother of the dead cub was still guarding the carcass it might be assumed that she committed the act and further conjecture gives a possible reason. It is known that the little bear had a head injury and could easily have suffered a leg injury as well when struck by the automobile. Perhaps the mother bear licked the wounds with intent to help him and, once tasting blood, could not stop there but ate away all damaged portions and carefully buried the parts as later found. It is doubted than an alien bear, for example the adult bear, would have taken the trouble to hide the pieces with probably constant harassment of the angry sow.

1957

Destructive Sweet Tooth
Roger Contor, Park Ranger

A recent article in the "Journal of Wildlife Management," concerning animal damage to the redwood forests in California, bring to mind an observation made by Park Naturalist Biddulph and myself on August 6, 1951.

We were hiking into the headwaters of Crow Creek from Sylvan Pass when we noticed several dozen freshly damaged trees in one comparatively small area. Typically, a large strip of bark (from a few inches in width to the entire circumference of mature trees) would be peeled off from a point three to five feet from the ground right down to the base of the tree. Puzzled at this, we determined to find the cause.

We soon noticed that only Englemann Spruce trees were being damaged, although the forest was a rich mixture of Lodgepole Pine, Whitebark Pine, Alpine Fir and the damaged spruce species. On the exposed trunks a small series of lightly etched grooves could be seen, but not other distinguishable marks. The lack of claw marks made me reluctant to agree with Lowell's suggestion that it was a bear's work.

So we continued on our hike, discussing the condition as possibly the job of porcupines, beavers, bears—even "Mallet-tailed cats." This discussion went on as we reached the glacial cirques behind Hoyt and Avalanche Peaks, and might well never have been settled if Lowell hadn't been on his toes as we came back through the area in question later in the day.

I was looking for a hermit thrush that we had seen on our way up when I heard a peculiar ripping noise and stopped; Lowell grabbed my arm and silently pointed into a grove of nearby spruce. There was the culprit at work. A black bear was busily pushing his nose and tongue up and down the freshly exposed trunk of a large Englemann. The stripped bark lay at the tree's base like withered flower petals, and the bear was lapping at the trunk as if it were a candy stick.

In a moment our presence was known and the animal slipped out of sight; but the problem was solved. After grabbing a bite of bark and tearing it down to the ground, the animal would press its incisors into the cambium region, forcing out and licking up the sweet, sugary sap. When one area was cleaned off, another would be exposed.

This apparently isn't a "common" practice, and fortunately so, for this one animal certainly raised havoc with a healthy stand of spruce in just a few days.

Social Life, Survival Skills, and Sizes

Here is a potpourri of other observations, some of which help to flesh out the early portrait of bear life. What I find pleasant about the format of *Yellowstone Nature Notes* is that no observation, however brief or disconnected from any bigger picture of life in Yellowstone, was considered trivial. Thus, dozens of little tidbits of information grew into something far greater and more informative.

1928

How Fast Does a Black Bear Climb?
William Rush

Recently (June 1, 1927), while I was riding along one of the little-used trails near the north boundary of the Yellowstone Park, my horse snorted loudly and, planting his front feet firmly together in the trail, came to a dead stop.

Glancing down the steep hill, along which we were traveling, I saw, about fifty yards away, what had surprised my mount. An immense black bear was standing on his hind legs and reaching up his full length on a fir tree. He immediately came down on all fours on hearing the horse snort and looked carefully all around to see what had made the noise. He even walked a step or two to look behind the tree. For a full minute he peered intently in all directions, but as both my horse and myself remained perfectly quiet the bear did not see us, and stepped back to the tree.

He looked up into the tree again, then all around once more. Apparently satisfied, he reared himself on his hind legs and started to scratch on the rough bark, evidently seeking a firm hold to begin the ascent. Having found just the grip he wanted, he gave a mighty spring and scrambled up the tree to a height of thirty or thirty-five feet with an astonishing rapidity that I do not believe a pine squirrel could have equaled.

Having attained his objective, which was some large limbs of the tree, he straddled one limb with his hind legs and, with his front paws resting on another limb, lay his shaggy head down on his paws and promptly fell asleep. Water was dripping from his fur, which indicated that he had just come from a bath in a nearby mud wallow.

My horse was apparently as intensely interested as I and did not move a muscle during the performance. When I was certain that the bear was asleep, I carefully dismounted and started down the hill for a closer view. For the first twenty-five yards I crept along very carefully, making hardly a sound, then in some awkward way I dislodged a small rock and down the slope it went, making a horrible clatter.

Bruin was awake at the first sound and watched the progress of the rock down the hill very intently. I, of course, stood absolutely still and waited so until the bear laid his head down again, which was perhaps in a minute or two, although it seemed five or ten minutes.

The old fellow did not go to sleep again, however, but was lying there watching to find out what was disturbing his rest. At my first slight movement he raised his head again, wide awake and angry when he saw that a man was near. Quickly getting to his feet on the limbs he made as if to start down and I, not wanting to race a big black bear that had just shown me his pine squirrel speed, withdrew from the field.

My horse probably marveled at the agility I demonstrated in getting back up the hill and into the saddle.

1930

The Challenge
Phillip Martindale, Ranger Naturalist

The night of June 26th at the bear feeding grounds at Old Faithful — while about 1000 people were seated during the lecture on wild life — a large grizzly lost his control of an area which he had held for a number of years. "Scarface," a bear that I named on account of one side of his face being torn and both ears missing, and an immense old grizzly, has really been monarch of this section and all other bears gave him the right-of-way. In fact, his thousand pounds of power did knock a large black bear about ten feet off from the feed platform last summer.

On the night mentioned, three bears were feeding when "Scarface" came down out of the woods. A large dark silvertip was there, and before "Scarface" had arrived within 100 feet of the feed platform, he left and started his almost human challenge. A swagger, both front and rear — moving toward his enemy of no doubt other encounters. This same swagger was used by "Scarface" but he circled away and kept his distance until finally he was chased out completely. When this happened the audience saw something that I had previously mentioned might happen. The victor came to the nearest tree, reared on his hind legs and measured his full length against the tree — a new commander of the area among the male grizzlies.

Concentrating the bears at feeding grounds apparently increased the number of aggressive interactions between them. This gathering of grizzly bear sows and young occurred at the Canyon feeding ground (notice the fencetop in the foreground) in the 1930s. National Park Service photo.

The bear "Scarface" came in the next night very early - alone - secured one piece of meat - watched the woods closely, and left— not to return again with other bears. He has lost—too old.

1930

A Bear Tragedy
Fred T. Johnston, Park Ranger

A little black bear that was caught in the Yellowstone Canyon this summer caused as much excitement as any of the "Grizzly shows." He was about three years old, and somehow climbed down into the canyon on the west side close to the lower falls, but was unable to get back to the top of the canyon wall and to safety. The people hiking along the Artist Point Trail on the other side of the canyon first noticed him, and immediately reports started coming into the Ranger Station as to his plight. An investigation was made in great haste, and an attempt was even made to try to assist the unfortunate bear in getting back to safety. Ropes were brought to a place where he might have been assisted, but he decided to move on at just that time, and it was deemed a fruitless expedition.

But he still remained on the canyon wall, and each day the crowds watching him from across the canyon became larger and larger. On the fourth day, however, he really showed the amount of nerve that a bear has. On each of the proceeding days he had tried his best to find a way out of this veritable prison, but had always seemed afraid to go down towards the river and the falls, which offered a chance of escape as it seemed to us. However, the pounding of the falls and the steep slope to the river would test the nerve of any animal, and he preferred to keep walking around at the base of the cliffs close to the top of the canyon. On the fourth day, no doubt being aided in his decision by hunger, he made his way to the bottom of the canyon right below the falls and, instead of going down stream to a place where there was a possibility of safely swimming across the river and climbing the other side of the canyon, he started to climb up the face of the cliff next to the falls. This, of course, was the climax of the show to the people watching from the rim of the canyon. The surprising part of it all is that he was able to climb up to a point even with the top of the Falls. Here he slipped when a rock came loose, and slid and fell back into the canyon, and then down into the river under the falls.

The whole tragedy was watched with intense interest and sympathy by many tourists, and the nerve of this bear as well as the struggle he made are incidents that those tourists as well as I will never forget.

1937

The Speed of Grizzly Bears
William E. Kearns,
Assistant Park Naturalist

Mr. Anderson and his family were driving toward the Cooke entrance of the park and were beyond the Buffalo Ranch. In rounding a curve near the Devils Well, a female grizzly and her two cubs were seen feeding on a carcass near the road. There were two cars preceding the Anderson car and the road was muddy with considerable slush snow in it. As the cars approached, the mother grizzly charged and jumped down into the cut made by the snowplow in recently clearing the road, but for some reason, just before the cars reached her, she sprang back up on the snow bank at the side of the road. While she was in the cut, her cubs disappeared over the hill into Soda Butte Creek. When the mother regained the bank and failed to see her cubs, she immediately gave chase to the cars which were then about fifty yards ahead of her. A brother of Mr. Anderson, who was riding in the rumble seat of the six cylinder Oldsmobile, became alarmed and warned the Ranger by rapping on the rear window. Vigorously blowing the horn, the Ranger tried to get the cars ahead to speed up all that they could, but due to the condition of the road, much speed was impossible. The grizzly quickly overtook the cars, and then jumping up on the snow bank, lunged out and down at the car. Several attempts were made in this manner to catch the car, but the grizzly missed each try as she lost time in jumping up on the snow before leaping for the car. Needless to say, the Ranger's brother had crawled down into the back of the car and had closed the rumble cover! They were chased from the Devils Well to Hoppe's Prairie, a distance of approximately two miles, and the maximum speed (remembering road conditions) was 28 miles per hour. The bear had just come out of hibernation, which must also be considered.

District Ranger "Ben" Arnold has reported further evidence on this question of speed of grizzlies. While the Arnolds were driving from Mammoth to Tower Falls one night early last summer, four grizzlies, a mother and three yearling cubs, were seen in the road ahead of the car at a distance of about two hundred yards. The bears immediately turned and ran down the road for a full half mile before dashing up the hill into the timber and out of sight. For the last quarter mile, they averaged 30 miles per hour and were not crowded at all. The bears were running on the oiled road, and did not have the advantage they would have had on a dirt surface.

We have had reports of grizzlies making 35 miles per hour when running before a car, but as I have been unable to verify any of them with a written statement, they shall be omitted.

Knowing the nature and disposition of the grizzly, no sane person is going to pursue and crowd one in a car, for fear that the animal might turn and demolish the car and perhaps, the occupants, too. From the foregoing incidents as cited, it is seen that speeds have actually been recorded for the grizzly up to and including thirty miles per hour with the bear setting his own pace. What they might be able to do under "pressure" or in anger is entirely a matter for supposition.

From observing grizzlies and having seen them, starting from a standstill, hurl themselves with tremendous speed upon an approaching rival, there is little room in my mind for the thought that they are "slow moving creatures." Grizzlies are powerful beasts, and as evidenced by the aforementioned reports, have considerable endurance, for covering two miles at from 25 to 28 miles per hour proves a stamina that would certainly try the best of horses.

Perhaps, after the roads are plowed open this spring, some obliging grizzly may run a faster heat, or some fool-hardy individual may crowd one to nearer the maximum, whatever that may be, but until such time, the best speed for grizzlies in Yellowstone, which I have been able to find, is thirty miles per hour.

1938

A Climbing Grizzly
Rudolf Grimm, Park Ranger

There had been evidence of the presence of a bear in the vicinity of my quarters for several weeks. Overturned garbage cans, dug-up marmot dens and tracks bore testimony to this. Also, several of the branches of the apple trees growing in the yard were found torn off, but this was at first blamed upon the numerous elk that daily feed here until some of the higher branches and finally the crown of the trees were noticed to be demolished. This, of course, was recognized as the work of a bear, especially as the trunks of the trees bore claw marks. The visits of the bear occurred entirely at night, and consequently we did not get to see him, but since black bear are not uncommon in this vicinity, it was assumed that the animal was of this species of the bear family.

On the night of November 3 there was a skiff of snow on the ground and a bright moon was shining, making out-door objects clearly visible for a considerable distance even from a lighted room, when, casually glancing out of the window, a large and small bear, presumably mother and cub, were observed ambling apparently aimlessly at a distance of approximately sixty yards from the house. All at once the cub made a dash for the vicinity of the apple trees and was followed somewhat more slowly by the larger bear. A number of deer that had been feeding under the trees took fright at the approach of the bears and ran off. The bears passed within forty feet of where I was standing, and I positively identified them as grizzlies by the very prominent hump on their shoulders and by their mannerisms.

For several minutes the two animals fed upon the apples lying on the ground. Then the older and larger bear raised up on her hind legs, gazed up into the tree, and dropping down on all four legs again, approached the trunk. Rising up again, she climbed it by grasping a limb about five feet from the ground, pulling herself up and stepping with her hind feet like a man climbing a tree, her progress at times obscured by the foliage, she ascended until her head and shoulders could be seen in the very crown of the tree. She vigorously shook the branches and apples cascaded to the ground from the loaded tree, and the cub immediately busied himself with the fruit. The brightly colored apples were clearly visible on the snow, and they were seen to disappear as if inhaled from in front of the grizzly's snout.

The old bear would pause for an instant as if to rest, with front legs and paws stretched at right angles from her body and over the branches presumably in order to better distribute her weight (estimated at 500 pounds) as her roost was none too secure at that height, only to again resume the shaking of the tree. In the course of this performance branches as well as apples were dislodged. This went on for about ten minutes, but a rap upon the window pane made the cub instantly alert and caused him much uneasiness, which was manifested by nervous running around and away from the tree. Finally the old bear descended the tree in reverse manner, but when she reached a point about eight feet from the ground she released all hold and slid down. She immediately raised up on her hind legs and looked about, but finding nothing amiss began feeding on the apples, the cub joining in the feast. However, the latter evidently had not recovered from his scare and appeared very nervous. He soon walked off and was followed a little later by his mother. However, looking out of the window later that night, both bears were again seen feeding on apples, though the older bear was not observed climbing the tree again.

On the following day a measurement was taken from the highest point in the tree reached by the grizzly, and it was found to be twenty-one feet. At this point a branch was broken or bitten off, and also a small amount of fur was found clinging to the stump of the branch. Limbs three inches in diameter were lying on the ground, and several of these had the appearance of having been chewed or twisted off. Claw marks were found on the trunks all the way up into the top of the tree, but it is presumed that these marks were made by the bear in its descent rather than in climbing. These claw marks have the form of straight and vertical scratches, running parallel with the trunk of the tree.

It has often been contended that a mature grizzly cannot climb; however, I have decided to no longer subscribe to this belief, and should it ever be my lot to have to climb a tree in order to escape from a grizzly, I shall take great pains to avoid apple trees.

1939

Marathon Swimming
for Black Bear
Wayne Replogle, Ranger Naturalist

Earlier this season I made a motorboat trip from West Thumb to the Southeast Arm of Yellowstone Lake and during the trip I had the opportunity to observe a black bear making a long distance swim.

We plied through the strait at Breeze Point and curved southward near the shore toward Wolf Point. As we moved along I was attracted to a Grizzly running at a good lope southward away from the approaching boat. He soon fled into the woods and out of sight. In order to avoid any sand bars we moved lakeward about a quarter of a mile when I gave my attention to Dot Island. Some distance between my boat and the island I saw an object in the water. We turned and motored toward it, slowed down to about three miles an hour, and much to our amazement we discovered a black bear making his way to Dot Island. He was at that time a mile or more from Wolf Point and at least that far from Dot. As our boat drew near he became a bit more excited and seemed to desire to turn on us, but finally he headed directly north to the north shore of the Lake. We followed near until he reached the shallow water at which

A black bear swimming the Yellowstone River, 1931. National Park Service photo.

time he scrambled up the bank and away into the forest. I would judge that the bear swam a distance of about five miles. This incident may give some light on bear migration and may lead us to believe that the bear has great endurance.

1948

How Much Do Black Bears Weigh?
Walter A. Kittams, Park Biologist

Too often we think in terms of the unusual, feeling that exaggeration is necessary for emphasis. This applies to impressions of the size and weight of Yellowstone bears. Anthony, in his *Field Book of North American Mammals,* gives the weight of the black bear as "200 to 450 or 500 pounds." Striking the average within that range is rather difficult because weights vary considerably with sex and age.

When eight bears were killed in early September of 1947 because of their habits of injuring visitors, I was able to make measurements of some mature females and cubs. Park personnel and many visitors became well acquainted with these bears, not only through their begging habits, but because of the injuries to humans attributed to them. If these bears can be remembered well enough to use them as guides in judging the sizes of other bears, the following data might be useful.

Bear	Sex	Age	Weight	Total Length
#1	Female	Mature	237 lbs.	52 in.
#2	Female	Cub	75 lbs.	39 in.
#3	Male	Cub	82 lbs.	40 in.
#4	Female	Mature	235 lbs.	57 in.
#5	Male	Cub	75 lbs.	38 in.
#6	Female	Mature	227 lbs.	56 in.
#7	Female	Cub	80 lbs.	39 in.
#8	Male	Cub	87 lbs.	41 in.

Two of the families, represented by bears No. 1 to No. 5, "worked" the highway about four miles west of West Thumb. The scene of operations of the other family was about midway between West Thumb and Lake Junction. Probably this coming summer there will still be evidence in the form of food wrappers and cans at both of these locations to remind us of them. Numerous tourists could not resist rewarding the beggars with food in spite of regulations which prohibit the practice.

All three members of the first family, No. 1 to No. 3, were very fat as would be expected at this time of year. The canine and incisor teeth of the mother were chipped and well worn, indicating that she was relatively old. Perhaps she was inherently a small bear, having a length of only 52 inches, and added weight as she became older as some people do.

The bears of the second family were in excellent condition though the mother did not have the reserve of fat which the other two mature females had. Probably the cub of this group enjoyed the company of a brother until late July. An automobile critically injured a cub in that vicinity, and rangers acquainted with this family were quite sure that he belonged to that group. The excellent condition of her teeth indicated that the mother was relatively young, but her weight and length rate her as full grown among the three adults. Perhaps she would have added several pounds in later years if man had not infringed upon her existence.

All three bears of the third family, No. 6 to No. 8, were brown in color. The canines of the mother were chipped and somewhat worn, placing her between bear No. 1 and No. 4 in age. She was in fair condition, and her cubs were very fat.

We might consider the cubs to get some idea of their growth and variations with sex. Peculiarly cub No. 5 was among the smallest in weight and length. Even though he had been without the competition of a brother or sister for six weeks, he was relatively small. This raises the question, do single animals benefit through additional care and food in comparison to twins? In both families which had a cub of each sex the males were larger in length and weight than the females. The two female cubs averaged about 78 pounds, and the three male cubs averaged about 81 pounds. At the age of about eight months the males are already larger than the females.

The weights given in the preceding table should not be considered as exact live weights. The measurements were made a day after the bears were killed; therefore an allowance would have to be made for loss of blood and desiccation if comparisons were to be made with weights of live animals. The weights as shown are sufficiently accurate for most uses. If we remember that those three mother bears averaged 233 pounds and the five cubs averaged 80 pounds in late summer, we can evaluate the "whopper" stories about huge bears.

1950

The Size of Grizzly Bear
David de L. Condon,
Chief Park Naturalist

During the summer of 1942 it became necessary to adopt control measures on grizzly bear in the Lake area in order to provide safety to the people visiting the park and stopping at the Fishing Bridge, Lake and Bridge Bay campgrounds. Several grizzly bear were killed and at that time I carefully measured and weighed a number of the animals immediately after they were killed. The results of these measurements were of unusual interest and I have kept them in my notebook pending an opportunity to prepare them for publication.

In measuring the animals a steel tape of good flexibility was used and a series of uniform measurements made on each individual. A set of Fairbanks platform scales was obtained and a plank deck large enough to hold an animal was fastened to the platform so that accurate weights of individuals could be secured.

The statistical information on size, in accordance with the measurements made on each individual and other information on them, is as follows:

Date killed	7/8/42	7/10/42	7/11/42	7/11/42	7/12/42
Sex	male	female	female	female	male
Tip of nose to end of last vertebrae	76½ in.	67 in.	68 in.	66 in.	77 in.
Elbow to tip of toe	22 in.	22 in.	17½ in.	16½ in.	20 in.
R. hind foot−width	6 in.	5¾ in.	5 in.	4½ in.	6 in.
R. hind food−length	10 in.	9½ in.	7½ in.	7 in.	11½ in.
R. front foot−width	6½ in.	5½ in.	4½ in.	4 in.	6 in.
R. front foot−length	7½ in.	6 in.	5 in.	5 in.	9 in.
Head width between ears	9¾ in.	10 in.	9 in.	10 in.	10½ in.
Head length	14½ in.	13 in.	15 in.	14 in.	12 in.
Height front shoulder	39½ in.	43 in.	39 in.	33 in.	41 in.
Height rear hip	38 in.	34 in.	37 in.	31 in.	36 in.
Girth around neck	32 in.	30 in.	29 in.	28 in.	34 in.
Girth around chest	51 in.	52 in.	55 in.	45 in.	55 in.
Weight	497 lb.	346 lb.	340 lb.	375 lb.	590 lb.

The male killed on July 12, 1942 was considered to be an exceedingly large bear and required the combined efforts of four men to lift him around so that measurements and other information could be obtained, yet it will be observed that this bear weighed only 590 pounds. The short broad head of this bear was of considerable interest for he presented almost a pug nosed appearance and his head length and width were a definite contrast with others. The skulls of all of these bears were damaged when shot, but have been saved for study.

The females all fell within the three to four hundred pound range, yet they were all mature and in two instances old animals. The female killed on July 10 had three cubs. She appeared to be a very old animal, all of her teeth were worn down and many of them were mere stubs. She had at sometime suffered a severe injury and had a very bad scar along her left hind leg where there was an extensive area of scar tissue and no hair growing. The females killed July 11 showed no abnormal characteristics, their teeth were well rounded and from their appearance they were animals well past maturity. Both of these were the mothers of two yearling cubs each and the cubs were running with the mothers at the time they were killed.

An adult grizzly bear at a dump in the last years of open garbage pits, 1967. National Park Service photo.

If the sizes and weights of these animals can be considered as representative of the grizzly bear, the animal is not as large as legend and our own imaginations might lead us to think.

1944

Epilogue
The Bear's Reaction to Man
Olaus J. Murie

Olaus Murie's 1943 study of Yellowstone bears was a milestone event in Yellowstone bear history. Not only did it provide a more comprehensive biological profile than had existed before, it also gave managers a great deal of good advice on how to change management practices to restore the bears to a more natural state. He proposed truly divorcing bears from garbage, which he said was completely unnecessary for the survival of the bears. He recommended additional research, not only into the natural history of Yellowstone bears, but also into ways of keeping them apart from human foods. Unfortunately, the study was completed during World War II, when funds for implementation of Murie's suggestions were low and when public interest in seeing and feeding bears was still high.

Murie's observations (excerpted from his 1944 report) on bear habituation to humans and on the impossibility of breaking bears from the garbage-feeding habit, seemed a nice conclusion to this collection, because he gave abundant warning of the perils of continuing to treat Yellowstone's bears like residents of some huge outdoor zoo.

But though his report had little immediate effect, I see it as a symbolic turning point. It could be said that with Murie's study, Yellowstone bear management began to pass from its era of relative innocence into a more informed period. Bears were less often seen as harmless woodland creatures

A Yellowstone bear jam, 1957. National Park Service photo.

and fuzzy tourist attractions, and problems that had been tolerated as nuisances were more often recognized as serious and potentially dangerous. Yellowstone was still a long way from dealing with its bear management problem, which we seemed to only dimly realize was as much a people problem as a bear problem. But as World War II ended and park visitation skyrocketed, the wisdom of Murie's words became more and more apparent.

It has been a long and painful road from then to now, with the bears at the center of one of the greatest wildlife management controversies in American history. The bears have been restored to something that more nearly resembles a wild state, and there is reason to hope we can keep them that way, despite ever-growing threats to the habitat they depend upon. But the spirit of Murie's message is still valid. The bears that inhabit the park and the surrounding wildlands can only endure if we understand and respect them, and they can only be as wild and free as we are willing to let them be.

The bear situation in the Yellowstone is by no means unique. The bear problem is not confined to national parks, but is national in scope. Wherever man enters the bear habitat for any length of time, bear-man relationships are bound to become complex. It is true, however, that this relationship has become most acute in the Yellowstone because of man's long residence there, the great concentration of people, the protection of bears, and the attitude toward the bears assumed by park visitors.

But speaking more generally, bears are likely to make themselves familiar whenever they find camps in their domain and are given encouragement by the presence of garbage or unprotected food. The bear problem has appeared in several national parks. Bears also become familiar around lumber camps, or any construction camp in the woods where garbage becomes available. I have seen published accounts to the effect that many bears become pets at the construction camps along the Alaska Highway.

Thus we have a broad picture of bear reactions, on the basis of nationwide experience. The outstanding feature, as I see it, is the tendency for bears to become quite tame and to lose their fear of man when they come in contact with him frequently. Animals in general have this tendency, of course, but some respond more readily than others. The bears seem to lose all fear and reach the point where they are not unduly alarmed when hit with sticks or stones to drive them away, or when shot at, or otherwise harrassed by irate campers who have suffered bear depredations. The bear retreats far enough to get out of the way, then goes the rounds seeking new advantages.

Tourists have this in common too: They seem to lose all fear of bears. Perhaps there are two reasons for this. Familiarity with bears poking along the highway like bums seeking a handout, or coming to the doors in camps eternally seeking garbage, tends to dispel any previous impressions of a heroic or dangerous animal of the forest.

Secondly, we must remember that over a period of years the bears of Yellowstone have been publicized, not as a wild animal in a wilderness setting, but as a picturesque "highwayman" begging from automobiles. Always there has been the implication of an animal seeking alms from man, always associated with automobiles, highways, camps. It seems to me that this is conducive to a viewpoint that the bear of the Yellowstone is almost a domestic animal, not to be feared. The bear becomes more or less associated with the humanized Three Bears of nursery days, safe within the covers of a book.

This is not the whole story, to be sure. The picture is much more complex. There are in addition the appealing characteristics of the bear itself, its interesting habits and mental traits. We know that the bear has endeared itself to mankind from earliest times. This is too big a subject to cover here, but the points I have mentioned above as applying to Yellowstone Park in particular I think are well worth keeping in mind. I think they help to explain the recklessness with which uninformed tourists take liberties with an animal which, after all, is not domesticated and really is a powerful and dangerous creature at close range.

All of this is well known by the Yellowstone Park personnel, but is worth stating here for the complete picture.

SUGGESTIONS FOR FURTHER READING

I hope this book whetted your appetite for more reading about bears. If so, here are a few suggestions.

There are a few other books about the bears of Yellowstone. I have already mentioned my book *The Bears of Yellowstone* (Roberts Rinehart, 1986). Others that are completely or partly about Yellowstone's bears are Milton Skinner, *Bears in the Yellowstone* (McClurg, 1925); Bill Schneider, *Where the Grizzly Walks* (Mountain Press, 1977); Frank Craighead, *Track of the Grizzly* (Sierra Club, 1979); Thomas McNamee, *The Grizzly Bear* (Knopf, 1984); and Doug Peacock, *Grizzly Years* (Holt, 1990). In these few books you will find a startling variety of opinions about bear management, a fair number of adventures, and a wealth of information about bear ecology.

There are scores of other bear books that are broader in their coverage. Among the most helpful and widely respected of these are Tracy Storer and Lloyd Tevis, *California Grizzly* (University of California, 1955); Andy Russell, *Grizzly Country* (Knopf, 1967); Adolph Murie, *The Grizzlies of Mount McKinley* (National Park Service, 1981); Steve Herrero, *Bear Attacks, Their Causes and Avoidance* (Nick Lyons, 1985); Paul Shepard and Barry Sanders, *The Sacred Paw: The Bear in Nature, Myth, and Literature* (Viking, 1985); and George Laycock, *The Wild Bears* (Stackpole, 1986). Some of these have been reprinted in paperback.

The best source of information on bears is the scientific literature, which is vast. Several of the books listed above have sizeable bibliographies of technical papers and reports, which should get you started in reading about bear science.

SOURCES

Note: Because many of these stories were extracted from longer narratives, they were originally untitled. Some titles in this book do not appear in the originals, but were created for this collection. In addition, selections are dated according to the occurrence of the event described rather than by the publication date of the description. Some of the selections from *Yellowstone Nature Notes* are excerpted from longer articles.

Part One

"Park Bears" appeared in Philetus W. Norris, *Annual Report of the Superintendent of the Yellowstone National Park to the Secretary of the Interior for the Year 1880* (Washington: U.S. Government Printing Office, 1881), pp. 40–41.

T. A. Jaggar, "Death Gulch, a Natural Bear Trap," *Appleton's Popular Science Monthly*, February 1899, pp. 1–7.

"The Death of Wahb" is from Ernest Thompson Seton, *The Biography of a Grizzly* (New York: Grosset & Dunlap, 1899), pp. 147–167.

"Bear Life in the Yellowstone" is from Theodore Roosevelt, *Outdoor Pastimes of an American Hunter* (New York: Scribner's, 1905), pp. 347–351.

"A Photographic Expedition" is from William Wright, *The Grizzly Bear* (New York: Scribner's, 1910), p. 163.

Part Two

"The Bear that Got Away" appeared originally in the *Helena Gazette* but is reprinted here from Nathaniel Langford, *The Discovery of Yellowstone Park*, ed. Aubrey Haines (Lincoln: University of Nebraska Press, 1972), p. 68.

"A Washburn Grizzly Hunt" is from William Pickett's extended memoir in *Hunting at High Altitudes,* ed. George Bird Grinnell (New York: Harper & Brothers, 1913), pp. 66–69.

"A Charging Grizzly" is from Philetus Norris, *Report upon the Yellowstone National Park, to the Secretary of the Interior, by P. W. Norris, Superintendent. For the Year 1879* (Washington: U.S. Government Printing Office, 1880), pp. 8–9.

"Tourist Attacked by a Bear" is a collection of four pieces: "Tourist Attacked by a Bear," *Wonderland,* Gardiner, Montana, September 11, 1902, p. 1; untitled news note, *Wonderland,* Gardiner, Montana, September 18, 1902, p. 1; "Warden Not Surprised," *Wonderland,* Gardiner, Montana, October 30, 1902, p. 2; John Pitcher, *Report of the Acting Superintendent of the Yellowstone National Park to the Secretary of the Interior* (Washington: U.S. Government Printing Office, 1902), pp. 6–7.

J. A. McGuire, "The Late Grizzly Bear Attacks in Yellowstone National Park," *Outdoor Life,* December 1916, pp. 583–584.

Ned Frost, "An Encounter with a Big Grizzly," *Outdoor Life,* December 1918, pp. 213–214.

"Bear Boldness" is from Milton Skinner, *Bears in the Yellowstone* (Chicago: McClurg, 1925), pp. 65–68.

Part Three

"A Bit of a Wag" is from Owen Wister, "Old Yellowstone Days," *Harper's Monthly,* March 1936, p. 476.

"Bears in the Yellowstone Park," *Forest and Stream,* October 6, 1894, p. 288.

Addison Neil Clark, "Bear Studies in the Yellowstone," *Outdoor Life,* August 1909, pp. 145–152.

"The Grizzly and the Can" is from Ernest Thompson Seton, *Wild Animals at Home* (New York: Grosset & Dunlap, 1913), pp. 216–218.

"Midnight Sallies and Outrageous Nuisances" is two letters to the editor of *Science,* June 20, 1913, p. 941, and July 25, 1913, pp. 127–129.

"Holdup Bears" is from Stephen Mather, *Report of the Director of the National Park Service* (Washington: U.S. Government Printing Office, 1919), p. 172.

E. J. Sawyer, "Ranger Treed by Grizzly," *Yellowstone Nature Notes,* September 1927, p. 6.

"The Lady Who Lost Her Dress" is from Horace Albright, "Harding, Coolidge, and the Lady Who Lost Her Dress," *American West,* September 1969, p. 32.

Phillip Martindale, "Close Contact with Grizzly Bears," undated hand-written report, Yellowstone National Park Library.

E. J. Sawyer, "Grizzly Visits Snowshoe Cabin," *Yellowstone Nature Notes,* November 1924, p. 2.

"Tracking an Old Grizzly" is from Milton Skinner, *Bears in the Yellowstone* (Chicago: McClurg, 1925), pp. 87–91.

E. J. Sawyer, "Bears Become Bold," *Yellowstone Nature Notes,* October 1927, p. 7.

Dorr G. Yeager, "Bear Steals U.S. Mail," *Yellowstone Nature Notes,* October 1929, p. 5.

Marguerite Lindsley Arnold, "Five Too Many Grizzlies," *Yellowstone Nature Notes,* November–December 1937, p. 51.

"Bears Behind Bars" is from William Rush, *Wild Animals of the Rockies* (New York: Harper & Brothers, 1947), pp. 31–40.

Part Four

Curtis Skinner, "Bedroom Life of Bears," *Yellowstone Nature Notes,* September–October 1933, pp. 1–2.

John F. Aiton, "More Denning Bears," *Yellowstone Nature Notes,* September–October 1933, pp. 35–36.

Herbert T. Lystrup, "A Grizzly Den," *Yellowstone Nature Notes,* September–October 1933, p. 37.

William E. Kearns, "Hibernation of Bears," *Yellowstone Nature Notes,* January–February 1938, pp. 6–9.

Wayne Replogle, "Canyon Bear Apartments," *Yellowstone Nature Notes,* August 1949, pp. 19–20.

Dorr Yeager, "Bringing Up Barney," *Nature Magazine,* January 1933, pp. 27–30.

E. E. Ogsten, "Adoption Among Bears," *Yellowstone Nature Notes,* August 1930, pp. 53–54.

A. Brazier Howell, "The Black Bear as a Destroyer of Game," *Journal of Mammalogy*, February 1921, p. 36.

Ben Arnold, "Cannibal Bear," *Yellowstone Nature Notes*, August 1930, p. 54.

J. Thomas Stewart, Jr., "Some Bears Get Their Share of Fish," *Yellowstone Nature Notes*, March–April 1933, p. 11.

Adolph Murie, "Some Food Habits of the Black Bear," *Journal of Mammalogy*, May 1937, pp. 238–240.

Lester Abbie, "Grizzly and Bull Elk Battle," *Yellowstone Nature Notes*, May–June 1942, p. 31.

Thomas Thompson, "Grizzly Bears Get Food," *Yellowstone Nature Notes*, May–June 1942, p. 33.

Earl M. Semingsen, "Grizzly Bear in Pelican Meadows," *Yellowstone Nature Notes*, January–February 1947, pp. 7–9.

Harvey B. Reynolds, "The Law of the Wild," *Yellowstone Nature Notes*, July–August 1950, p. 44.

Joe J. Way, "Survival of the Fittest," *Yellowstone Nature Notes*, July–August 1951, p. 46.

Thomas F. Ela, "A Unique Case of Bear Cannibalism," *Yellowstone Nature Notes*, January–February 1954, pp. 7–8.

Roger Contor, "Destructive Sweet Tooth," *Yellowstone Nature Notes*, January–February 1957, p. 7.

William Rush, "How Fast Does a Black Bear Climb?" *Journal of Mammalogy*, November 1928, pp. 335–336.

Phillip Martindale, "The Challenge," *Yellowstone Nature Notes*, September 1930, p. 61.

Fred T. Johnston, "A Bear Tragedy," *Yellowstone Nature Notes*, October 1930, p. 1.

William Kearns, "The Speed of Grizzly Bears," *Yellowstone Nature Notes*, January–February 1937, pp. 2–3.

Rudolph Grimm, "A Climbing Grizzly," *Yellowstone Nature Notes*, November–December 1938, pp. 58–59.

Wayne Replogle, "Marathon Swimming for Black Bear," *Yellowstone Nature Notes*, September–October 1939, p. 55.

Walter A. Kittams, "How Much Do Black Bears Weigh," *Yellowstone Nature Notes*, March–April 1948, pp. 17–19.

David de L. Condon, "The Size of Grizzly Bear," *Yellowstone Nature Notes*, January–February 1950, pp. 5–6.

"The Bear's Reaction to Man" is from Olaus J. Murie, "Progress Report on the Yellowstone Bear Study," typescript in the Yellowstone Park Library (1944).

About the author

Paul Schullery is the author, co-author, or editor of many books on nature and outdoor sport. He has worked in Yellowstone as a ranger-naturalist, as park historian, as a research consultant, and as a technical writer. This is his fourth book about bears, the previous ones being *The Bears of Yellowstone, American Bears: Selections from the Writings of Theodore Roosevelt,* and *The Bear Hunter's Century.* He currently works in the Research Division in Yellowstone and teaches a "Grizzly Bear Ecology and Management" course for the Yellowstone Institute.